As always
Ben
with
much
thanks
Ben

Ivan Tunnel ends *Dream Catching Canada* with this email to his friend Pete.

Here it is

To:	Pete
Cc:	
Subject:	Here it is

Hey Pete. As promised. Many thanks, and Happy New Year,

Your bro,

Ivan

ps now it's time to rant

And with that the reader completes a six month journey that begins on July 1, 2017 – the 150th birthday of Canada – to the clock striking midnight, 31 December 2017. What comes inbetween those two dates is an unprecedented literary excursion into the heart of Canada's colonial darkness and ends with a question for the reader, a question posed before deep time once again swallows all of Canada, all of history.

Ivan Tunnel's first work of fiction is the sort of surprise you get when you visit a mysterious-looking bookstore and stumble upon one of the most unique books you will ever read. It tackles a crucial subject – in this case, Canada as a colony and Canada as colonizer – and by extension the tragic footprint of Empire everywhere. And Tunnel does this in anything but the expected way.

Dream Catching Canada is not an essay, or treatise; nor is it political philosophy or anything one might strictly call *Canadiana*. Indeed, it is at times very raw, giving voice to politically incorrect views and sentiments running through Canada today, while capturing in poetry and images the dignity and refinement of Canadian indigenous cultures from which all Canadians have benefitted. And while it is very much a story focused on several Canadian characters and themes stretching from 12000 years ago to the dawning of the first day of 2018, it speaks to colonized people everywhere; and to modern colonizers.

We are fortunate that Tunnel's work has moved from his earlier non-fiction accounts of topics on war and peace – important and often set in far-off lands – to a masterfully-crafted fiction that takes place in Canada: a story that should be read with a mind open to a slightly gonzo style of mixed media writing, and the poetic treatment of the subject in a manner similar to Ondaatje's *The Collected Works Of Billy The Kid*. I recommend *Dream Catching Canada* be taken in manageable doses and digested slowly. For there are many layers here and in Tunnel's typical manner, just when perpetual darkness seems inevitable, he provides us with a glint of hope, some light in the darkness of deep time.

Edmund Bartholomew Edwards

Essayist and Literary Critic

There descended a
great darkness the blue-blackness of it
suffocating the light, the thin outlines
of man and beast indistinguishable;
the birds now silent – a
great sleep spreading, drugging
all –
all tricksters, merchants,
players – all finally silenced,
finally quiet; the churning mind,
the unfulfilled hope,
the whispered prayer also giving way
to an unfathomable, peaceful sleep.

From there, from primordial
thick dreams we wake
each reaching, groping in the
early light.
Separating from the meld
turning our faces upright,
warming and yearning;
cared for by halflings,
well-meaning creatures sprung likewise
from the dark
caught in mid-life
knowing only how frail
the new ones are and how
broken the old ones have become.

Reaching down to us while
crooked-necked from years of
upward strain – having
tried to read the signs –
becoming all there is and was,
fulfilling their
destiny, refusing now
to dream lest they
sleep again before their time.

And all they
have to offer is
their struggle, some guidance
and a stubborn hope
that they and you
and others yet to come
learn the lessons of the
moon and the sun
and watch, contented, as
the darkness once again descends.

So if you ask me what to do about the Indians...

Nobody asked you, asshole.

No, seriously, I'm not joking this time – and what's with this asshole
stuff? We are brothers, man: bro and...

You started the asshole thing, Not me. Not me bro.

OK, OK. So I know this isn't politically correct bro, but...

No buts about it.

IF you ask me...

OK, Pete, My Bro, what should we – Canadians –
"do" about the Indians, meaning Canadian Aboriginals or
First Nations or our Indigenous people – what?

Well, I'd get rid of them.
I mean I'd just get rid of the reserves
Because they are a failure and if the Indians or the Government
think that they can go back in time to their traditional way
of living – hunting and gathering – living off the land –
it's a pipe dream. It's bogus.
There's no way. Even if the deer and the fish and the animals they
trapped or the buffalo or the whales and seals they killed and lived off
were there – and they aren't or for sure won't be before too long –

they don't know how to live that way and they wouldn't want to

anyway.

Get real.

They love hockey on TV.

Some of them love casinos and gambling and even trips to Vegas.

Their kids are killing themselves

because those little isolated reservations they live on

are incestuous, boring places for kids who are plugged in,

plugged in just like kids everywhere

with their tablets and Facebook and they look around at the shit

and nothingness of the 'rez' and

they've been fucked over by their

drunken fathers or uncles or whoever

and it's a horrible destitute place

and the reservations should be closed down and the families

dispersed and assimilated into Canadian culture.

That's what I think.

And I think a lot of people think it too but

won't say it.

Like saying it means you're

racist.

Means you don't give a shit.

Means you're a red neck asshole, Bro. Asshole.

You serious?

Yah, I'm serious.

But what about the wrongs done to them? Like the whole
colonization thing? They were, and as far as I can tell
are still being slowly and steadily ground down. Like
genocide on the installment plan.

I'm saying those reservations where they are like Third World
countries –
no drinking water, for Christ's sake. Moldy houses. Dogs they can't
afford to feed running wild,
garbage everywhere, no civic pride, no employment for any of the
young people who might want a job.
A welfare, sick, dependent existence –
somebody should admit that they are obsolete.
Just like hundreds of other ghost towns all over Canada.
They were vital. They had a purpose: mining, logging and milling,
fishing and canning operations – and they just ran out of steam.
Technology changed, even a new highway passed them by – there was
no more need for what they cut, or dug, or milled or processed there –
and they died.
The people there left. They moved on.
The ghost town was left behind.
The reservations are the same.
It's not racist.
It's not lack of compassion.
It's realism.
In fact, it's real compassion to say, 'Hey, look, you people had a raw
deal. Wrongs were done.'

Big wrongs!

Yah, OK, big wrongs.
But there's no way you can go back and there's nothing
for you on the reserve.
Others everywhere all through history
and others now, driven from their land without a thing –
Syria for example –
you know what I mean.
But who has the balls to say it?

What about the harm done? This was their land. They had
their own languages and culture. It seems that most of
them befriended the white man. The Hudson's Bay Company
agent, the white explorer. The fur trader. Even the
Christian missionaries…

Well?

Well?

Well, there must be some way to pay them off. Settle the score.
And move on.
And not keep playing this bullshit game that they are going to restore
their cultures. That they are going to live separate lives on some cut-
off, useless tract of land.

Not so useless – at least many aren't. There's still natural resources there. And many have never surrendered their rights to their traditional territory.

Yah, yah. I hear you. So if there's a Treaty, Canada and the Provinces should honour it. If there isn't one, there should be. Get it done. Figure out what's owed and help them leave their hopeless reservations and take their money and integrate – if you like that word better – into mainstream Canadian culture. And if there are a handful of viable communities because they still have some resources and there's employment and a reason to keep the village or whatever going – fine. But not as some sealed-off Indian community run under some sick arrangement set out in the Indian Act where there are elected chiefs and hereditary chiefs and no clarity and in-fighting and dysfunctionality and it's just really a big fuck-up as everyone pretends they can live with one foot in the past and one barely in the present and go into the future 'reconciled' and 'revitalized'.

So these places become ordinary municipalities just like all the others? That's what you think?

Yah and they thrive, change, wax and maybe wane and disappear just as any other one does.
That's what I think…

But do you know that some of them, many, have been in treaty talks for years – like 20 years. Or have been trying to have the score settled, as you say, for

infringement of their rights – meaning being ripped
off by the Government of Canada – rights backed up by
rulings from the Supreme Court – and those talks just
keep grinding on. Do you know that?

And in the meantime the fish in their territory have been
overfished by commercial fisheries, their forests have
been cut and every last tree sawed, or worse, shipped as
logs to the States or China; or the minerals underground
have been mined. All to the tune of billions of dollars.
Billions for the white man.

It's no accident that paying them to keep talking,
paying them to dwindle on their reservations, setting
up an inquiry or a commission to look into the Indian
'problem' from time to time is a helluva lot cheaper
than paying them for the real value of what they have.
Or for what they had and was taken by big business and
the Government while all the talking went on.

Like I said. The whole current approach, as Canada celebrates its
150th birthday, is bogus.

To run as fast as the wind

To hear the earth pounding beneath your feet

To jump flying through the air

To hit the other side running

To run crazy with the dogs

To feel strong and wild and free

To see the herd far off

To smell the herd on the wind

To faintly hear the drums at home

To be swallowed by the great big sky

To run and run and fly

To know the hunt is coming

To be chosen by the tribe

To feel the tribe's anxiety

To hear the drums beat slowly

To feel the steady pounding of your heart

To be prepared by the old ones

To become a buffalo

To be taught every detail

To keep your hide on and stay low

To move slowly to the front

To keep your eye on the jump stone

To wait for the moment

To feel the herd erupting

To take the lead

To never look back

To jump just far enough

To wait until the end

To have the herd arrive

To be fitted with the hide

To smell the animal oil smeared on you

To feel the hide's weight

To be reminded of every detail

To have the tribe embrace and dance around you

To feel their hearts enter you

To wait

To hear the stirring of the herd nearby

To be prepared by the old ones

To be seen off by the tribe

To leave the tribe far behind you

To enter the wild herd

To stay low

To wait

To hear the drums getting louder
To smell the herd
To stay low and move like a buffalo
To sense the herd's anxiety
To hear the drums now louder
To hear the snorts and stirring
To move in front

To wait

To remember all the details

To wait

To hear the tribe yelling
To hear the drums pounding
To hear the herd moving
To remember every detail
To run to stay in front
To hear the tribe screaming
To hear the drums pounding
The hoofs behind you

The stampede coming

To run, run

To remember every detail

To hear the herd upon you

To be the wind

To smell the herd upon you

To run and run and run and

Jump!

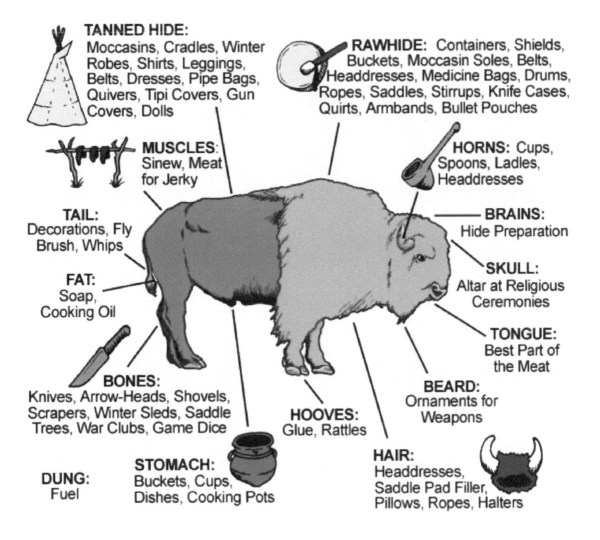

TANNED HIDE: Moccasins, Cradles, Winter Robes, Shirts, Leggings, Belts, Dresses, Pipe Bags, Quivers, Tipi Covers, Gun Covers, Dolls

RAWHIDE: Containers, Shields, Buckets, Moccasin Soles, Belts, Headdresses, Medicine Bags, Drums, Ropes, Saddles, Stirrups, Knife Cases, Quirts, Armbands, Bullet Pouches

MUSCLES: Sinew, Meat for Jerky

HORNS: Cups, Spoons, Ladles, Headdresses

TAIL: Decorations, Fly Brush, Whips

BRAINS: Hide Preparation

FAT: Soap, Cooking Oil

SKULL: Altar at Religious Ceremonies

TONGUE: Best Part of the Meat

BONES: Knives, Arrow-Heads, Shovels, Scrapers, Winter Sleds, Saddle Trees, War Clubs, Game Dice

HOOVES: Glue, Rattles

BEARD: Ornaments for Weapons

DUNG: Fuel

STOMACH: Buckets, Cups, Dishes, Cooking Pots

HAIR: Headdresses, Saddle Pad Filler, Pillows, Ropes, Halters

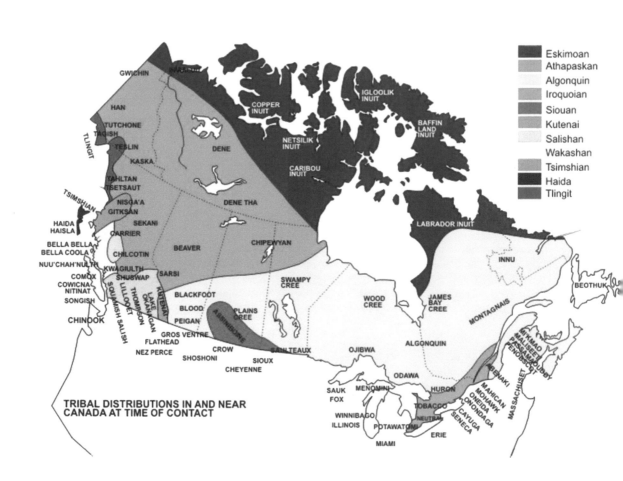

TRIBAL DISTRIBUTIONS IN AND NEAR
CANADA AT TIME OF CONTACT

A way off on the flat blue water under a soft layer of white cloud turning pink as the sun sets a huge thing has appeared, its white upper body lit up just at the edge of the earth, over there, far away and motionless

We gather at the shore, our safe shore where the friendly water laps gently in the cool breeze and see now that this giant is coming our way, growing bigger as the blue water darkens to deeper colder blue some black lines across it

No one knows what this floating thing is or if it is really there for it is a ghost thing moving without men with paddles, deathly silent and bound straight for us

Our Chief orders some young men to build a fire and sends other fast runners back to our settlement to bring the Old Man here

The fire is not for heat but to show we have power over fire and the medicine man is not for sickness but to deal with this ghost

We huddle together

The fire begins to roar

The children are drawn to the shore's edge and they are called back to stay behind us at the fire, waiting for the Old Man while the line of clouds thickens to a purple haze and the object grows larger, its white

top some hides or material tied to dead limbless tree trunks, its dark
bottom now curved like a huge canoe

The Old Man arrives with three drummers and the runners place
some of his special possessions under a tree back from the shore at the
forest's edge and they cover them with hides

Our Chief asks the Old Man if he sees it

We hear his hushed reply it is a vessel from another world and the
Old Man signals to the dummers who sit in front of the fire facing the
thing to start to drum quietly

Now the thing has grown so huge it blocks out the sky as the white
top falls down the trees

The Chief and the Old Man go to the shore's edge as we see many
small creatures lower canoes like ours into the water and begin to
spill over the edge of the vessel and into the canoes

They have paddles

They look like men, pale –

And they are coming our way.

Your Majesty, Medord des Groseilliers and I are honoured that you receive us,

Frenchmen from New France with a proposal

strange and of certain promise.

We come to ask you to command an enterprise

that will bear bounty for your Kingdom

not just for a few years, or a decade but an endless

future, so wild, exotic and unexploited is the land.

And just to give you an appreciation

of the varied and copious animal furs that the

country will yield — for choice fashion and comfort —

we have here a small display of

the finest beaver hides, otter, soft mink, and marten —

the beaver so plentiful that you will receive shiploads that

your merchants will sell not only in London but throughout Europe.

And now, if I may, we wish to tell you

of a truth known only to the two of us, having explored beyond

France's territory in the eastern and southern part of the New World.

The King waves his hand –

It is this, Your Majesty.

There exists far to the west and north of French-held territory

a vast land with more furs than all that trapped

to this day. A land we know exists only by the relations

we have with the Hurons and further west and north, the Cree.

These Natives are the enemy of the French, of the Iroquois

upon whom the French rely.

And they count us as friends and future trading partners

and look upon the English as honourable

and favour relations with the Great Chief of the English.

This, Your Majesty, is the most cherished truth we

share only with you and ask that you make swift the

formation of a company to exploit a territory far greater than the Dutch, who

are in decline, and the ambitious King of France, Louis the XIV, whose goals

in the New World you will destroy .

The King nods and raises a finger to proceed.

And we propose you name this company, which will rival and surpass the East India Company, the Company of Adventurers of England.

The King speaks:

And so Monsieur Raddison, is it true you were captured and lived among the Iroquois, with whom you no longer associate? Tell me.

Paul-Espirit Raddison replies:

Your Majesty —

The King interrupts:

And that you were tortured by these savages…

Raddison glances to des Groseilliers:

That was a long time ago, Your Majesty, when I was a boy.

The King nods.

I escaped from the Mohawk encampment where I had lived several months

with a family that had taken me when I was first captured

and I was recaptured with some others — we had killed

some Iroquois we met on our escape northward to Trois Rivier —

and they returned us to the Mohawk settlement and prepared us for torture.

If not for the pleas of my Mohawk father

I would have been tortured to death.

King Charles asks:

You credit your Iroquois 'father' with your life? What did they do to you,

a child?

Raddison:

He told me to be strong and to sing as they cut out my fingernails.

And for days as I was tied and pierced in the foot with a red-hot knife

I was to sing.

The King:

You sang?

Radisson:

I had to. They would have killed me like the others if I had not sung — to show courage — and if my father had not appealed to them. He was a good father.

The King:

And then?

Radisson:

And then I escaped again. Back to my Canadian home.

Afterthought

To:	Pete
Cc:	
Subject:	Afterthought

Hey Pete,

Great party Bro! What I remember. Once the fireworks and shooters started I think I was MIA. Jane says I really blew it. Mooned the neighbours. Geez, sorry bout that. Anyway, thanks again. And was just thinking about your politically incorrect view of what to do about the Indigenous people. Apart from this sense that there's a real colonialist bias built into the way that is framed – like they are the White Man's Burden – and how the real answer should be what they say they want (assuming what they say is realistic from any point of view) – it's pretty complicated when you start to think about how the process of integration would take place, assuming they agreed with you that the current situation is not viable – the reservation system and the way they are governed and the non-viability of anybody really being able to go back in time etc.

Anyways, I know some Indian communities that have resources and seem to be getting along OK. And I was thinking about what if the others were really paid a fair amount – spread over years I guess – for the resources that were exploited by outsiders, and they continued to have ownership of the resources on their traditional territory – wouldn't they be able to be 'viable'? I mean, I know many little towns that seem to exist as bedroom communities, or places where mainly retired people live and with their pensions and savings – and there's nothing else going on in them, and they seem OK. I know some Indian communities are as small as 80 people on rez and maybe another 80 already off rez, and I know one that has about 1500 on and 1500 off and if 'the Crown' said in negotiations, "Here's the money you are owed, and a) invest it or divide it any way you want among your people but the *quid pro quo* is you have to move and integrate because there is no future here in what is in effect a ghost town, economically speaking; or b) if you choose to stay – for whatever reason – there's no more support you will receive after a 'phase out' period: your community will be treated just like any other small community in Canada." Wouldn't that be both fair and realistic?

Sometimes I think there's just this sick co-dependence between the Crown and the Indigenous people of Canada.

The colonizer and the colonized.

How to cut this two-way umbilical cord? This perverse co-dependence.

Maybe I'm overthinking the whole thing.

Ivan.

His Majesty King Charles 'the second' was a merry man at Court,
A bon vivant so liberal for his times – a wife and seven concubines –
With many did he consort;
It was business as usual, the mere flip of a hand, a sip of claret –
That for a paltry ten pounds paid in gold
In 1668 he leased Bombay to the East India Company and
By a series of five charters he then did grant
The Company with rights so extensive
His Empire to unfold.

When Radisson and des Groseilliers, such entrepreneurs as they
Were, charmed Charles with stories and samples of fur,
He once again looked for someone worthy on whom to bestow
Governance of a coming colony, the strange wealth and expanse
Who could know.
Thus in 1670, by Royal Charter, control of the Hudson's Bay basin
Was given to the Hudson's Bay Company and the territory named
Rupert's Land after his jolly cousin Prince Rupert of Rhine, its first
Governor.
The British now embarked to explore and conquer paths west and
North and there, as Radisson had promised, they found
Savages strange
Wilderness pristine
Great rivers and lakes and – yes –
Furred animals that they trapped and slaughtered by the millions
So that money could flow from the new colony
To England, its favoured merchants,
The Monarch,
The CROWN.

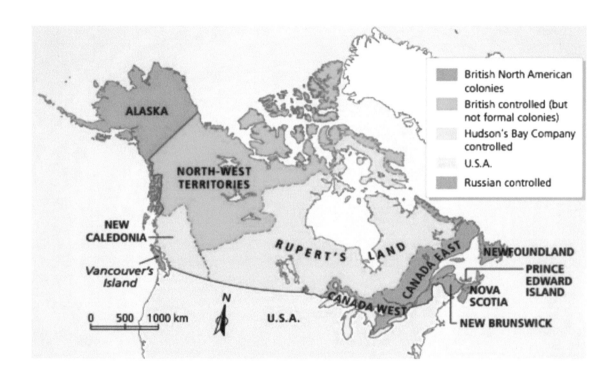

Snarled, wasted

wild and mystic, scrawny

jack pines and ponds,

creeks and

torrents—moose country.

Greens and greys and coal-black crevices,

lichens of lime,

mauves and blue—rock cuts, scrub brush—swamp.

Snarled, wasted

wild and mystic,

looking glass lakes

with poplars and birch

flickers and owls—moose country—swamp,

for miles and miles and miles.

I saw a maggot

And I watched it grow

It sprung from nowhere

That could be told

It arrived by boat on the east

And on the west

And it came to the far north too

By different means – on foot,

In canoes, on sleds.

It was so foreign –

There were times

It looked friendly, curious and peace-loving:

Other times it was hostile

And full of

Poison.

Mostly it was arrogant,

And destructive.

It fed on its host

And looked for more food

As it grew and took on its true colours

Its multiple personalities:

Braided Uniforms, Robes, Top Hats.

And we the host – trading with it, teaching it how to survive –

Suffered to near extinction.

Indeed it seemed determined to

Kill, obliterate that which

Gave it life.

Not just men, women and children

But the land upon which we stood

And on which we dwelt.

We had fought before.

We had raided, and battled and stole

From one another.

We knew conflict, skirmishes and

War.

But we had no standing armies, no police,

And our weapons were tools for hunting and

For survival – not made to kill

Another man, not to blow up

A whole settlement.

So some of us fought this alien thing.

This maggot that was

A hydra unfolding,

Still thin and desiring to bloat itself.

To become

All.

Sometimes

Our great physical strength

Our knowledge of the land

Our skills of survival

Our strategies of battle

Our clever tactics

Our courage

Our bravery

Our passion for survival brought us to a stand-off,

Sometimes to treaties made or treaties promised –

But often we could not prevail.

And so many of us had died by some plague that we were

Already beaten down, weak, and could put up little resistance.

The maggot grew.

It had great deceptive powers

It had done this sort of eating before.

It started most often with an open hand –

To trade.

Then it built forts and settlements

Where we assembled to exchange our furs and our catch

From the sea.

The guns it offered us, the fire water,

And the supplies and intercourse

Lured us and intoxicated us and weakened our sense of who and what

we were.

When it took us by force

When it drove us off our great land

When it confined us

When it exhausted our natural resources

When it stole our children

When it forbade our potlatch

When it scrubbed our language from our mouths

When it took away our names

When it raped our women

When it killed our warriors

When it humiliated our Chiefs

When it made a mockery of us

When it stripped us of our spirit

The White Man had succeeded in making us their 'Burden' –

their non-white subjects

in their colonial possession,

in a vast settlement

now known as Canada.

What I did not tell King Charles was that the
Mohawks ate the hearts of brave men to avail
themselves of their bravery. Thus I sang only
so much. And that Des Groseilliers and I had
made the same proposal to Louis XIV.

Paul-Espirit Radisson

The thick bush

was heavy with clouds of blackflies we inhaled, choking. Spitting. Breathing

through our sweat-soaked collars.

We had left our horses days ago

and by canoe

had paddled the big river west and then north

over speeding rapids and past jagged rocks,

limbs of spruce clawing,

threatening to skewer us.

Until the waterway had split.

We chose a path, portaging now through deep bog the swampy water up to our knees

our mukluks sucking sounds as we pulled our heavy legs out, again and

again and again.

Past the lethal narrows

we slashed

into this endless, dense brush;

mosquitoes tormented us incessantly,

our blood caking on

any exposed flesh

while we fought off huge meat-eating flies

stumbling forward, slashing and

marking the trees,

piling and scarring rocks

driving stakes

making borders.

While overhead clouds grew heavy

in a vast sky

our bodies ached beyond ache
the drug exhaustion took over
as the pale shadows grew long
and then the rain started,
and we were forced to stop.

This was our duty:
to map this inhospitable Godforsaken land.
Name places.
Imagine that waterways could be divided,
nomadic natives confined to one area.
Carve up nature as if the land can own the sky and the water,
and an Empire own it all.
Make it the
Crown's Territory.
Make it the Dominion of Canada.

It was 1864 when Great Grandfather Wilhelm arrived, a German immigrant fleeing Bismarck's wars and economic hardship. He and his wife Caroline were careful to speak no Yiddish, and with their two-year-old Pauline went by horse-drawn wagon to follow the colonization road and find the wild acreage he had obtained in Wilberforce. There they set to work to carve a homestead from the forest, a hovel for them and a few animals before the deep cold winter set in; and in the spring broke their backs picking rocks and digging a garden plot, securing their place in the new world.

That second winter Pauline died and their first son, Benjamin, was born. Two more were to follow. Three boys to work the land, help cut the timber, drive the mighty Belgian draft horses through deep snow, build a new log cabin and grow into proud and independent men.

Wilhelm then began his healing arts
in that remote German settlement.
His daughter-in-law – and apprentice – Lydia, went with him into the meadows
and forests to collect the healing plants: camphor, chamomile, plantain, and
the powerful chaga mushrooms.

Sometimes he and Lydia went out at dawn so that the dew was on the leaves,
sometimes when the blooms had failed and
the roots were dug out of the stubborn ground.
The blackened chaga they had to hack and saw from the yellow birch.
And on the crude wood burning stove in his log cabin they prepared the
ointments, brewed tinctures using alcohol he had distilled in the summer kitchen,
and tied some plants upside down to cure the buds and dry the leaves.

He and Lydia – now a midwife – tended to the sick with preparations:
mustard plasters, bread poultices,

hot and cold compresses,

medicines from nature.

And Lydia had special powers, psychic powers that Wilhelm
acknowledged but did not understand.

(above) Squared log house

(opposite) Scoop-roofed shanty

Her name was Commosung.

She did not know that for some it was 1500 AD and that her people had been here for more than ten thousand years.

Her tribe followed the food: fishing and gathering what they could use.

And here they built a shelter against the rain and winds that would stir the great water that seemed to start far across where white tops showed on the huge rockies.

The longhouse felt safe and smelled good to her.

They would be warm and full in this season of rain and cold.

The Old Man, however, had stopped leaving the shelter weeks ago.

He no longer searched the shoreline for shells or sat in a happy trance in the blowing rain as the waves crashed on the craggy rocks.

Now he whittled a small branch of the tree they had collected when they were here before.

His breathing had grown heavy.

His energy so low.

She would leave now and find the tree and prepare the medicine.

The powers of the tree would go into the Old Man once again.

This time the powers did not work.

The Old Man grew small and his energy retreated.

He stopped eating the best fish she could give him.

He drank only water from his special shell.

Then he stopped drinking.

His energy was so very low.

The chanting began.

The drums beat slowly.

She shook the rattle slowly.

He left his body.

The longhouse went quiet.

The strong men wrapped his body in the skin of the giant fir tree.

They placed it in a canoe and the big water took it away.

She would carry the twig he had carved.

She would take care of the medicine.

Chief of the Songhees would agree in 1864 that the

settlement they had built hundreds of years ago in now-named

Victoria Harbour, where they traded with the Hudson's Bay Company,

could be relocated.

Furs they trapped.

Fish they caught.

Seals and sea otters they caught.

Traded for guns, blankets, cooking utensils, and liquor.

Not all would be moved, as some of the Tribe had stayed away from the

settlement.

Trappers mostly lived in the bush.

Fishermen lived as they always had, in sheltered places along the coast.

The Tribe did not think of territory. Their traditional territory.

It was the land.

They were one with it.

Now, in Victoria, the potlatch was outlawed.

Now no more than four Songhees were allowed to meet together on the street.

Now their land was being transformed so they could not recognize it.

Nevertheless, they moved and

Soon they would be moved again, to Esquimalt,

The place of shoaling waters.

And a young warrior, Cammosung's great grandson ten times removed, and a few

Braves took siege of the Hudson Bay post.

They fired some shots from their rifles.

They held their spot.

Then cannon balls blew them away.

In 1869, for the bargain basement price

of 1.5 million dollars, the Hudson's Bay

Company's claim in Rupert's Land was

sold to Canada and its legal monopoly on

the fur trade was officially ended in 1870.

Afterthought

To:	Ivan
Cc:	
Subject:	Afterthought

Hey Ivan,

You know you take everything very seriously and we all love you anyway.
Seriously.

The problem is, what the hell can we really do about it? About the Indians in
Canada who have been fucked over. About the Syrian refugees. About Trump!
Empire has a huge nasty footprint, my friend!

We get to vote, which is great. And we have to hope the people we put in do the
best they can, knowing of course how politics itself is so influenced by big bucks
and pushes and pulls from all directions.

Anyway, let's get together for the Grey Cup game. It's looking like my Alouettes
don't have a hope in hell, and your Lions really suck, bro.

Pete

William Beacham (Indian Agent NWT)

December 25, 1883

Christmas Day! Having arrived here mid-December with my wife Thachiwan and child, I officially commence my duties on January 1, 1884.

The post is well-established and outfitted com more than comfortably for the few employees here; and the quarters for my family are quite acceptable. Everyone seems welcoming, some curious that I should have as a wife an Indian woman. Although she does not speak Cree and will not easily play the role of interpreter and liaise with the Cree as she did in the south with the Sioux. Yet her presence is a sign that I value the Indian. That good relations matter and auger well for peace commerce and peace among all concerned. And I did not reveal that I lived among the Sioux after being captured from my family, and yet this has not gone unnoticed. This knowledge preceded my arrival.

I believe my experience and the word of it will help clear the way for a better life for those whose longstanding way of living is rapidly coming to an end. This land is changing so quickly. I have my assignment, and I shall execute my powers under the Indian Act with the utmost respect for the Indians in my area of responsibility, which is vast.

\<no subject\>

To:	Pete
Cc:	
Subject:	\<no subject\>

Hey Pete,

Guess you heard Gord Downie of the Hip died. Just 53. What a bummer. I wasn't a fan but I liked a couple of their tunes that celebrated Canada like Bobcaygeon, and Courage. He sure got some praise in the States as a combo of Springsteen, Dylan and ? And it was cool that he rallied near the end to bring the Aboriginal reconciliation issue to the forefront, although I never heard any specifics about how that would happen. And I'm not sure that Trudeau's focus on reconciliation – now the missing women's inquiry – or maybe it's just a commission without any real teeth – will really amount to a hill of beans.

It's strange sometimes how things just seem to come together or how a pattern of sorts can appear in our lives. Like Jane was trying to sell our mobile kitchen island and a First Nations guy bought it and when he came to pick it up we got talking – said he was from ONT. I thought he was Mohawk and he was – way out here in Victoria – and he's married to a Cree from northern Saskatchewan I think he said, and he's working on Indian self-government, land management specifically. Says that it's just that specific part of self-gov he's on and I said maybe this is a delicate question but do you really think that the goal of s-gov is realistic. And he said sure, it's a long term process for many Indian communities but he has seen some really doing well and I said it seemed to me most of the whole fed gov system is set up to keep them talking and not much really solid was happening and he said yah Canadians talk about the 20 billion dollar a year Indian problem but the Department of Indian Affairs was a big monster. He seemed so enthusiastic about his job and the prospects for Indigenous people and I wished I could share that optimism for getting past colonialism…

And then yesterday we took the grandkids to the ballet. It was Dracula. Really cool. Lots of people in costume in the audience with Halloween on Tuesday and we were sitting in the theatre and Jodi pointed out the gilded box seats – about three on each side suspended above the stage and asked what they were. For some reason – maybe because it is Victoria, British Columbia, I said they were for royalty at one time, and I may have added and the wealthy people.

Anyway, I was nearly floored a few minutes after. The place was full. The artistic director had said his intro and then said now all please stand for the entrance of the Lieutenant Governor of British Columbia, so and so - a woman. And I really felt like just sitting there. And everyone stood up and I was hesitant and thought hey don't embarrass Jane and the kids and just play the game. But it was like WTF. It's the 21st century. It's the 150th birthday of Canada and we still have this horseshit about the Crown in England. We are still a colony ourselves. We still have an umbilical cord that costs us $55 million a year. $55Mil!

And I don't care about how much people like pomp and ceremony. Or how the Queen/ Monarchy somehow reassures these monarchists, provides stability etc etc.

Anyway pretty clear to me that my father was right when he used to say "poor Canada". I never really knew why he would say it. But it's starting to become apparent. Like we can't stand on our own two feet.

Distill alcohol and mix in chewing

tobacco, red pepper, soap, ginger,

molasses and red ink.

Highly addictive.

Cheaply made.

Trade with Indians for buffalo robes,

furs, horses and anything you want.

April 30, 1884

These past four months have been unremarkable here except for the activities of Louis Riel and the reverberations in my jurisdiction. The Indians are indeed upset, as are the Metis. So there is tension among ~~them~~ and, to some extent, between them. And there is anger towards the Government of Canada for introducing so many settlers and for promises unfulfilled.

Thus we await anxiously Ottawa's man who is being sent to teach the Indians to farm. He is to bring implements with him and this will be none too early.

September 26, 1884

September and the snow has begun to fall.

A few Cree arrived here looking very rough, saying their encampment is in dire straits. They ~~accuse~~ rightly accuse the Government of failing to give them the tools for farming, and without the buffalo they have no food or robes or adequate moccasins for the snow, and only a few tepees that will be able to withstand the winter.

People have begun to die and they asked me where the food rations are that the Government promised when they signed the Treaty. So Dr. McKee — a young doctor for the NWMP who just arrived here from McGill University — and I are leaving in the morning, taking them back. Although two are quite infirm and will stay behind.

I could not tell them there is no food, despite my appeals to Ottawa that there has been inadequate provision to assist them to become farmers, and the resources necessary to meet the promise of ~~looking~~ taking care of them during the transition (a transition, frankly, that is going to take decades, if it happens at all).

Grey Cup and another book

To: Pete
Cc:
Subject: Grey Cup and another book

Pete,

Grey Cup our place. November 26. We'll do wings and salads. You bring a dessert. K?

AND, I've decided to write another book. I know… but I feel compelled. I'm into it already. I'm drawing on our conversations (most of them anyway, ha) and giving myself a deadline of December 31, 2017. End of the 150th.

It's a fiction and I'll build in some of my own poems and shit. The working title is the Decolonization of Canada – or the Liberation of Canada. Something like that. Although it's not really only about that but that serves as a metaphor for what I think might be said about what it is that drives us. Or what we are missing. Do I have answers? Not likely. Maybe more a 'show don't tell' approach. That's what they always say, "Ivan, don't tell, show". It's a gamble. And I won't bug you with reading any of it 'til it's over.

Lions are out for sure. Go Toronto Go! If they make it.

October 4, 1884

Dr. McKee and I have just returned from a most disturbing scene. As we and our party approached the encampment we found nine bodies of the dead, decomposing, strung up in the leafless trees, as is their custom.

And those still living were in a depleted condition that will surely lead to many more dying this winter. For goodness sakes, most of their lodges are made of cotton only, not hides, and many of those are in a rotten condition. Their clothing is scanty, the elderly feeble and there is simply no food except the few small game they are able to trap or hunt on land nearly unproductive of that food source.

McKee did what he could and will report to his superiors. As will I. But I am constrained by the deliberate reduction of my discretionary power and centralization in Ottawa.

Fiscal cutbacks.

November 30, 1884

McKee visited last night and Thachiwan and I hosted him
to a meal of venison and an evening of conversation. He
is a fine man who has been kept very busy tending to the
sick, whose number increases. ~~Nos~~ Worse, he delivered
news in confidence that he will be leaving the NWMP
at the end of the year, when his contract ends. He is very
frustrated and will not renew it. He will return to Montreal
to establish a private practice. ~~His knowledge~~ That will
include some work on nearby reservations where his knowledge
of French and his insights gained in this one year will serve
him with the Mohawks.

He insists that the Indian Act is really a tool to assimilate
all Indians, and I ~~agree~~ have a hard time disagreeing.
Indeed, it is the ruthlessness and pace of that which is so
disconcerting. To wipe out so many cultures and make way
for rapid settlement.

February 1, 1885

McKee left for Montreal yesterday, January 31.
He remained a month beyond his contract to see a few
patients through. It was a sad occasion, I believe for him
as well as I.

February 20, 1885

Riel's political stirrings continue to destabilize relations
here, even so far north as we are. My work now requires
more attention to the settlers who keep arriving with great
expectations and who find the ground truly unprepared for
them. ~~Thus~~ So far there have been no open hostilities,
but I have put the NWMP fully on notice there
could be violence.

March 1, 1885

A reporter from the Manitoba Free Press has published an article on the condition of the Cree settlement McKee and I visited last fall. He found fully 50 dead in the trees and described it as ghoulish — which it must have been.

Winter has taken its toll, as I knew it would. ~~There are~~ The encampment has only two dozen still alive. The story attacks the Government and I am sure to be asked by Ottawa why this bad press could not have been avoided.

Meanwhile there is no increase in the paltry provisions I can offer the Cree. And some unauthorized fur traders are still at it with the firewater. The Cree are being destroyed without a gun being shot.

March 1, 1885

It comes as no surprise that the Cree have initiated violence — the bison population is in serious decline, and in an attempt to assert control over aboriginal settlement the Federal Government has violated the terms of the treaties signed in the latter part of the last decade. Treaty violation and rampant poverty has spurred Big Bear, a Cree chief, to embark on a diplomatic campaign to ~~change~~ renegotiate the terms of the treaties. The timing of his campaign coincides with an increased sense of frustration among the Métis.

March 30, 1885

Riel's rebellion was no surprise either. But the Cree's violence and Riel are not related. Riel and the Métis have been defeated, as I expected.

Continuing to watch this, and ~~appearing to co~~ by my silence appearing to condone Ottawa's conduct, is a most disturbing thing. I find it difficult to look Thachiwan in the eye and uphold my office.

William Beacham (Indian Agent – formerly – NWT)

July 25, 1885

The snow will begin as early as September. Another winter here is impossible for us. I cannot abide the hypocrisy. After many talks I will take Thachiwan and our son Jerome, named after my father, south. We will head to the Lake of the Woods. There, as a free man, I will return to my true calling: living in the wild, living off the land. The fur trade is far from what it was, but there is still a living to be made ~~there~~ as a trapper and a trader. Thachiwan will be close to her people. Thus I have tendered my resignation, much to the regret of the Lieutenant Governor and my colleagues here, who are indeed fine men.

And so my small journal goes with me, to one day ~~be~~ perhaps be of interest to Jerome. His short stay among the northern Cree.

William Beacham
Indian Agent (formerly) NWT

Grey Cup and another book

To:	Ivan
Cc:	
Subject:	Grey Cup and another book

WRITING ANOTHER BOOK??

You are unbelievable. I have trouble opening my mail and you have the drive extraordinaire.

K re Cup.

Reading a biography of Kerouac. Laurie picked it up at a garage sale. She complains I'm stuck in the past and keeps giving me stuff that keeps me there. Lol.

And not sure if you have heard this one:
Why were the Indians here first? They had reservations.
Put that in your book.
Not!

Later Bro.
P

When they were young and mated

They had watched the old ones

Quietly make preparations,

Usually grandmothers as so many of the

Old men died early,

Quietly getting some clothing together.

Quietly touching the young ones,

Saying nothing.

And when the time was right

They were left behind by the tribe.

Alone,

Forever.

And

To the white man this seemed

Selfless, and

Savage –

Something beyond,

Something peculiar,

Unchristian.

When in a far-off tribe

Many years later

A young man, a misfit who had become

A nuisance,

A young man

With beautiful long black hair,

Perfect white teeth

Smooth brown skin

Shy eyes

Was brought before the

Village Elders

He was banished from the reserve.

There was no energy or appetite or

Will to reconcile.

Six weeks later he was found dead

In his lonely room

In Whiteman's town.

He had blown his head off with a

Shotgun.

Hi-Heeh, Hi-Heh, Ho!
Hi-Heh, Hi-Heh, Ha!

So the Ojibwe Tribe chanted when they gave
Grey Owl his name:
Washaquonasin – he who flies by the night;
and when he met King George V
he raised his arm in salute saying
"How Kola" and in Ojibwe
"I come in peace, brother".

Hi-Heeh, Hi-Heh, Ho!
Hi-Heh, Hi-Heh, Ha!

And how many white men want to be
Indians so anemic they feel,
Their religion a pale substitute
for being one with nature, alive
with the stars and moon to guide them,
at home in the wild –
smelling, seeing, hearing, feeling
every pulse of mother earth
and the creatures thereon.

Hi-Heeh, Hi-Heh, Ho!
Hi-Heh, Hi-Heh, Ha!

What white kid has not wanted to be an Indian Brave

with long hair down his back,

war paint on his face,

dressed in leather,

feathers blowing in the air,

riding a steed barebacked

drawing his bow and

the tight gut

his raw power

transformed Into

a precise extension

of his being

hitting the mark

as though the arrow

his eye penetrating the target.

Hi-Heeh, Hi-Heh, Ho!

Hi-Heh, Hi-Heh, Ha!

What white man has not looked upon

the noble features of an Indian Chief

and wished his own visage and carriage

had just some of that

dignity.

Hi-Heeh, Hi-Heh, Ho!

Hi-Heh, Hi-Heh, Ha!

What white woman

has not gazed upon the Brave

and wished she were

in his care, felt the strength of his toned muscles,

opened herself

to his manhood

and slept contented in

his arms.

Hi-Heeh, Hi-Heh, Ho!

Hi-Heh, Hi-Heh, Ha!

Hi-Heeh, Hi-Heh, Ho!

Hi-Heh, Hi-Heh, Ha!

Hi-Heh, Hi-Heh, Ha!

(below) Thomas Moore (true name unknown)
before and after entrance to the Regina, Saskatchewan Residential School, 1874.

I am Mohawk, a man, and my name is Tehoronianhen. It means 'covered in clouds'. My name was taken away from me and now I am called something else. I am called William.

I am Mohawk, a woman, and my name is Katsitsaneron. It means 'precious flower'. My name was taken away from me and now I am called something else. I am called Victoria.

I am Siksika – Blackfoot in English. I am a woman and my name is Isapoinhkyaki – 'singing crow woman'. My name was taken away from me and I am called Mary.

I am Algonquin, male. My name is Aklanu – 'he laughs'.
My name was changed to David.

I am Algonquin too. Female. My name was Alsoomse – 'independent'.
It was changed. Louisa.

I am Cree and…

I am Inuvialuit, descendant of the Thule….

I am Heiltsuk –

I am Songhees –

My name is

I am.

Ghost
towns

Canada Harbour, Newfoundland

Nitchequan, Quebec

Balaclava, Ontario

Uranium City, Saskatchewan

Woodfibre, British Columbia

Children shouting always running

mothers sweeping and scrubbing, cooking and waiting for

fathers to come home from the ocean, the mine, the mill, the plant, the

factory

tired and hungry and proud to be making a living

growing a family

having a stake in this land

this wild frontier

this new world.

Saturday the place lights up

a day of fixing the house, filling the pantry, watching the kids

go crazy in the street, the neighbourhood smiling the

small and honest rewards of labour and dedication

a roast in the oven, pies on the counter

the whiskey and fiddle waiting

for the party to begin.

There's no place like home.

No place like here, right here at this moment.

No place better to put down your roots.

Sunday quiet

the rain is falling the snow is falling the ocean is grey the waves are

breaking on the rocky shore the sky is enormous the forest is dense the

windswept Prairie immense and

the silent spirit world

is everywhere in every form

and the kids want to go outside and play

the adults want to stay in

and make love.

Every family is in its

private world

in the home they have built

where they get swallowed by the timeless now.

Peace has descended on Sunday.

Monday, and **THE WHISTLE BLOWS!**

The fishery, the mine, the mill, the plant and the factory shout out: catch it, dig it, saw it,

ship it.

The school bell rings.

The kids run to school swinging their lunch boxes, tripping over their own feet.

laughing and teasing each other.

The village is growing expanding along the waterfront, into the bush, uphill

to overlook the splendour of it all. Progress.

A new dance hall a new hotel a blacksmith's shop a post office a barber
shop a second store a better road a new dock
a police station.
The church is getting a bell
there's a doctor here now.

Rumour has it that more families will be arriving soon.
From where?

Specialty men for the fishery, the mine, the mill, the plant, the factory. Settlers who want a
new start and DPs from the war. Adventurers whose imaginations have been captured by
the wild frontier.

The town is booming!

More men and equipment, more merchants and entertainers, more streets and houses.
Freshly washed laundry drying on the line. Gardens sown. Produce shared. There are
chicken coops in some back yards. A man at the edge of town raises pigs and makes the
best smoked sausage. The women have quilting bees. Kids grow up.
The boys get a job in the fishery, at the mine, at the mill, at the plant, in the factory.
There are weddings. Families grow into aunts and uncles, cousins and in-laws.
Some old people die. The community comes together. Someone's house burns down.
The community rallies.

The men go fishing and hunting and the women make huge meals
– a feast of the
catch, the hunt.

Music fills the air: the fiddle, a piano, a banjo, the spoons.

There is room for everyone.

There is more of everything.

Until the fish are hard to find, the catch small. The virgin pine and hardwoods cut and milled; the forests cleared. The gold rush runs dry. The price of nickel and copper and iron shift. The town's fishery, mine, mill, plant and factory struggling.

The town is nervous.

The Company closes leaving

another ghost town on the frontier.

And if you close your eyes and listen

you can hear the happy voices of children playing in the street and

wrapped in her husband's arms

a woman

crying at the threshold of

her empty home.

I can smell the Veneer Plant

That wet woody skunky smell hanging

In the air

And drifting over our hockey rink

On the Indian River just behind

The small houses here on

Moffat Street

I'm alone on the rink but Johnny is supposed to be

Coming out after his Christmas lunch

And I guess some of the other kids will show up too

Anyway it's really cold, about 30 below but the ice is so hard

And I can skate like the wind and

When the holidays are over we'll be playing against Our Lady of Lourdes

And I'm gonna score lots of goals and

Tomorrow night the Lumber Kings are playing

And I'll see some of those kids there and my

Brother Arlie will be in goal and

The Kings are taking on the Hull Valiants they're a tough team

They really can skate but we've got Tom Lesnick at centre and Barty Ball is just

Insane like clear the track here comes Shack and

The Pembroke boys coached by Brother Paul

Will beat them I'm sure then they'll have to take on Sacred Heart

And maybe there'll be a scout there from

The Chicago Black Hawks cuz

The Hawks were here before the NHL season started and I got to see them

In person and it was just amazing to see the Golden Jet Bobby Hull and Glen Hall

And Stan Makita and the whole bunch of them

Play at the Memorial Centre

And somebody said they were here because

The Lumber Kings are a farm team of the Hawks

And that means we are connected to Chicago and

They have these men who travel around and look for good players that

Are like grown out here on their farm

And they could go all the way to the NHL

So I could too I know Tommy Lesnick could and Arlie could too they are both

So good and maybe that big defenceman Briscoe I can't remember his name but

He's got a really powerful slap shot

I saw him drive one from centre ice right into the net

And I'm working on my slap shot too because I have a great wrist shot but you

Have to have more to make the NHL

And I'm not sure where Chicago really is

It's in the States

And all I know is

Everybody says all the hockey players in the NHL – Toronto Montreal Boston

Bruins (I like them too) New York – *the Rangers* – the Wings and the Hawks are all

Really Canadians playing even if the teams are in the United States

And we've got one kid at school, John's his name too, he's a nice guy but he

Doesn't play hockey I don't think he can skate but

Maybe he can I think I saw him trying one time on Highview rink anyway

He's from Texas or at least his grandparents live there because last summer at

The end of summer before school started

He came to my house and showed me these little bibles his grandma gave him

And they were really small in a box and he gave me a whole box

And asked me to give them to my friends

And he also gave me a fruit I've never ever heard about it he said it was a

Pommegranit or something like that I tried it and it was really strange

With these seeds and hardly any fruit

He brought it from Texas I think and he wore cowboy boots some time

And they were really weird

But he really is a good kid and one day when I was out by the highway I saw

The strangest thing

It was a big car,

A really big car pulling what looked like a long silver spaceship

Behind it.

And I told my brother Arlie and he

Said they are called Airstreams and I was lucky to see one because

Nobody in Canada has them they cost too much money

And my other brother Cal met another guy from the United States too and he was

From Texas too he said his father was at the Veneer Plant or something like that

One of the factories here maybe the Splint Factory or GE and he wanted to

Trade his sports car for Cal's Bonny and they did and Cal got extra

Parts with the deal I think it's a motor it's in the garage and a couple of other

Things and this guy – I saw him when they made the trade – seemed really shy

And I don't think they stayed around Pembroke very long but I know he got a

Really good bike that 500 cc double carb Triumph Bonneville which is made in

England and it won a big race in Daytona Florida

The sports car Cal got is a weird looking one but I like it

It's jet black with red carpeting all over inside with strange fins and Cal took me

For a ride and showed me how it has a 5th gear and it's a touring car and I was

Surprised when he said it's an Alpine Sunbeam and they are made in the States I

Didn't think the Americans made sports cars

But the United States is just so big and they've got great baseball teams and

Anybody who is really good in sports here in Canada really goes to the States

Where they get paid a lot

Like Bobby Hull and Bobby Orr, man is he good and he's from Parry Sound it's

Pretty far from here but in Ontario near Goderich I think and I played Goderich on

Our all-star team but they

Beat us out in the second round of the tournament right

Here at the PMC but we had done really good because we beat these really big

Guys from Ottawa – the Mintos –

They were big and had great uniforms and really nice equipment and when we

Were skating around before the puck was dropped I checked them out and

I just remembered what Dad had said about the bigger they are the harder they

Fall and I am a rushing defenceman like Bobby Orr and so I was determined to

Beat them –

And we did we all played so hard and even the pretty bad guys on our team

Maybe I should say the weaker players really put everything into it and they

Skated and passed better than I had seen them do and

We beat the Mintos as polished as they looked and I scored two goals in a 4–2

Victory and I plan on making it to the Kings and

To the NHL and actually I guess I'm with Orr because I'd rather play for Boston

Than Chicago even if we are their farm team and I like the Bruins' colours my

Uniform is the Bruins' colours and I wear the 'C'.

Jan, 3. 1958 **THEY LIKE IT COLD**

While the adults shiver and cuss old man winter, the small fry are having a ball as cold winds bring firm ice to Pem- broke. Skates and hockey sticks were out in full force this week as the youngsters took advan- tage of the combined cold weather and the holiday. Seen at Centre Ward school are John Kohls and Benny Hoffman.

Observer Staff Photo.

"Indians!"

It took a long time before we called them Natives –

    Natives: we don't yet know the depth of the word

        We haven't the roots, ancestry, the short and direct

           Link to the tribe

           to the earth, the sky, the wood

           the misty moss-covered forest, the

           clear, crisp hardwoods,

           the streams, the tiny brooks winding through oak and

           pine — trickling, building, feeding

Golden Lake.

Golden Lake:

Indians – Whiteducks and Jockos, Sarazans and Amikons –

    Algonquins…

Who dared go there!

From our distant Christian comfort we were horrified by

    "the Reservation" – God, it scared us as children,

    Our first real sense of other

           of alien

           of race.

Indians

On the Reserve

At Golden Lake.

So beautiful, so frightening – Golden Lake –
The Indians
The drunkards, fighters, viscous winos
Just over there, back of the village, on the lake –
Off the beaten track.

Who dared go there!

And there they stayed, in the main –
An occasional embarrassment as one might wander, drunken,
Near the railway tracks in Pembroke, by the trestle where
All drunks went.

And there they stayed, off the beaten track,
For years,
For decades,
On the Reserve –
Indians at Golden Lake.

Drunken Indian
slumped in the Drug Store doorway
other Natives nearby go about their
Native business in quarter-time never pausing,
worried about the Drunk.

The Drunk:
don't be concerned about looking over-curious no one
will notice – certainly not those frightening-looking Indians –
or the Squaw with the black eye, her pregnant 14-year-old daughter
by her side and
the Police
well they
just keep on driving by, never
bat an eye so
walk right up if you want and take a look at
The Drunk.

God!

His bulbous nose reddened and pitted if
you looked closer the little yellow seeds
of this strawberry might actually be there,
his lips are purple, bruised,
his dark hair dirty, oily and tossed, his
neck wide open his eyes rolling back his
saliva dripping thickly from a cut chin
his fingers are long his hands covered in a

loose brown-scaled skin;

filthy,

his clothes shoddy

he smells like vomit

he's rolling into the street awkwardly over

the cement steps to the Store – as a white woman

delicately

picks

her way around him.

This is the Native?

This is 'The' Native?

This is the Brave I've heard about

The noble race I've been told about

The silent man I've read about?

THIS IS GENOCIDE.

Missing and Murdered

To:	Ivan
Cc:	
Subject:	Missing and Murdered

Did you the catch the CBC news last night on the release of the Interim Report? Sounds like the concern we had about mandate and resources took up a lot of time but I caught that they are calling for a police task force to be launched now and I think I heard them say that about 1200 women and girls were murdered or unresolved missing cases between 1980 and 2012. That's like 40 a year for fuck's sake. But like all murdered women, most were murdered by men, and most of the men knew the woman. I had been thinking there was some kind of white predator types, even serial killer types preying on aboriginal women. Doesn't look like it. But I'm not sure of the stats so don't quote me. It's tragic any way you look at it.

P

This was his territory, the smutty
dingy hovel where Natives flopped
on broken furniture or played aimless
cards at the centre table.
This shack in Kenora. His territory, their territory.
Their tiny piece of ground on their expansive traditional land: the Indian
Friendship Centre.

Foreign and Alone among Ojibway and Cree, I was the minority
sitting meekly on a busted couch and watching him approach,
huge strides across the floor, towering over me,
I froze in Fear.
He bent, folding himself into the seat beside me; immediately
the stench of urine rose from him and smothered me.

He was a giant.
Huge muscular hands jerked some sign language
only he understood.
Then he tapped me, insisting, mumbling in broken
language – a garbled mix of Ojibway, English, and French – something very
serious,
something deathly.

I looked into his eyes.
Such soft brown eyes they were.
I nodded in agreement. And from that minute he shared his
broken tale…

Once in a while he would smile – laugh, then quickly recoil

under another wave of pain – deep indelible pain.

A fallen giant.

Could have broken me with one blow, instead he convulsed

his message.

A story of genocide: and I understood

how we are all victims.

Living, dying, dead

From cradle to grave

From ego to family

From family to tribe

From tribe to nation

And nation to empire

In our movement through time

We are held captive

To persons or places or whirligigs

Things seen and held in the hand or

Tucked away in secret stashes,

To things imagined or believed

So real, so real.

This private world

So strong

The need so strong

So much hunger for trust, for home

We obey that which we must,

From living to dying to dead.

The days are all mixed up

The months are too and I remember when

I was going full tilt there were times I woke up not knowing where I was – Atlanta,

Khartoum, back at

the lake in Ontario?

So I wasn't too surprised when I was told that today is Remembrance Day,

November 11 even though I

had taken time yesterday to pause in a sliver of sunlight by the grey ocean

to remember.

But what was I going to remember?

The names of wars?

The victims of Hitler's extermination camps?

The refugees fleeing Myanmar?

The rape and pillage?

That the five permanent members of the UN Security Council are the world's

biggest arms traders?

Remember what?

I stood still in the sunlit forest looking out across the ocean

seeing the waves crashing in, smelling the salt air, with

thanks for being alive and thanks for being free filling my heart.

And then the images came.

Jane's grandfather, wounded in WWI, never the same thereafter. A man so

peaceful who spent the rest of his life tending his strawberries,

pruning fruit trees, filling Grandma Bea's life with sweetness and light;

speaking seldom, speaking a humble wisdom when he did.

His brother Donald, killed in the same brutal war.

Two farm boys from Dunnville Ontario.

Evan and Don.

To kill or be killed in hand-to-hand combat.

One felled by a bayonet, the other wounded for life.

And I thanked them for giving me so much.

And my thanks spread to my uncles George and Joe who fought in WWII,

And to Bobby's dad who also was never the same

when he came home. A mixture of humility and alcoholic rage.

And the world stopped while I remembered them.

So it came as a surprise that

while shopping today at RONA, now another American-owned store – Lowes –

the announcement came that the eleventh hour of the eleventh day of the

eleventh month was

moments away

and would all customers please stop and take a minute in silence

for all those who had given their lives for

our country.

Hello?

Hey Cal, how you doin?

Ivan – it's good to hear from you.

And good to hear your voice too Cal. You getting ready for tonight's big game?

Well, Ivan, I lost most of my interest in it.

Really?

Yes, but I'll still watch the Senators even though I

don't know any of the players any more they keep trading them

and a lot are Russians or Swedes and I think the only

local name that kept coming up was Bryan Murray – you know he was from

Shawville and died not too long ago.

Yah, I recognize the name he really did well for himself.

And there's that Hoffman boy, he's pretty good.

Yes I haven't watched much this year I'm a pretty fickle fan

maybe for the same reason - there's no real local connection - but I plug in

around the playoffs and

it's hard not to cheer for the Sens especially when they gave

the Penguins a real run for their money.

Did they ever!

Really! Maybe they'll beat Syd the Kid and those lads tonight which would be nice for sure.

Yes it would. And to have a local Canadian team win the cup next spring. It's been hard to even get a few Canadian teams into the finals it's all about money these days...

It's entertainment Cal - how many teams are there in the league anyway - 18 or so.

Thirty one.

Thirty one! No wonder the Canadians can't make the playoffs!

Anyway, they really can play when you think about how we played…

Well they're faster, and bigger.

Bigger for sure.

And they've got really good skills.

Yah, but you were really good too.

So were you.

Yah I guess so. So who is this Hoffman?

He's from the Kitchener area. He's fast and shoots well.

Kitchener, eh?

Yes. I checked him out and he comes from another strain of Hoffmans.

Yah? Like where?

Maybe he's from the part that settled in Pennsylvania or in that part of the States.

I tell everybody at Tim Horton's we are related, way back, on my mother's side.

No way!

Yah, we might be… and it makes for a good story. You know I go to Tim's here every day and –

Right, with that old gang you have, right? The two old pharmacists?

Did you say they are in their late 80s?

No, no. They are in their 90s.

Holy geez. And they're still at it.

Yes, Ivan. I'm young by comparison.

Well you're not that old.

Getting up there.

What, you'll be 80 this year, right?

That's right.

Well that's great. You sound great. Strong.

And so do you.

I'm OK for sure. But those old guys, didn't you say they were still skating?

Yes, every Tuesday. We go to the rink here in Gananoque and skate. We have an hour but most of us just do about half that.

Well, just going round and round isn't much fun even though I love to skate.

No it's a little boring but good exercise.

Did those pharmacists play hockey?

No, not really. They came from the Prairies and went to school at Queen's University.

Huh —

Although one of the brothers took up skiing and skied well into his 80s.

Geez! His 80s —

And the other one took up flying. Had his own plane and kept it at his cottage on the St Lawrence near here in the summers...

So — I'm back to watching and I'll be watching for you in the roster tonight. You're lacing up, right?

Ha — that's right.

Good. And I guess you'll get the winning goal, sharpshooter that you are.

Yes. Maybe.

Well you better because Ottawa needs you. To go all the way.

Well, maybe I'll score it, or if not that Hoffman lad will.

Right on!

And if we beat the Pens tonight then maybe you guys will call me up and we'll both be playing whoever is next — and then for the cup!

Yah, probably some other American team.

Yah, right. Anyway. Let it rip tonight Cal.

Ok. I'll do that. And thanks for calling Ivan. It's great talking with you. To hearing your voice.

And with you.

Ok. Bye now.

Bye Cal.

Bye Ivan.

Bye.

I'm glad Jane is cheering for Calgary, guess Laurie doesn't care one way or another.

Well I don't really care either but I get your point. We need some tension here.

A little drama, right?

Ha. Right. Like there's no drama in our lives and we set some up by cheering for a team or like even right now Jane and I are watching The Voice.

Really!

For sure. I lost interest when the coaches, Adam and - what's his name - I keep forgetting.

Who? Blake?

Yah Blake… started acting like kids and I just thought I've got better things to do. You watch too?

Laurie likes it.

Right. So this year the talent's really great isn't it?

For sure!

So we really don't care that much who wins but we're looking for someone to back and I think we are heading towards that tall blond girl, even though the 15-year-old is so good.

No kidding, they're all really good this year – should be lots of the drama you are after.

Enough to keep watching. Our weekly dramatic relief. If there is such a thing.

Could be, should be.

Anyway, so just before you got here the Panel voted three to one that Calgary is going to win. And it's snowing like shit there.

Man, they can have it.

But you know, it's strange. They're saying it's shaping up to be a real Canadian Grey Cup classic because of the snow. Like without snow you aren't in Canada.

Fuck, they can have it.

Really! I kept looking out the window to check and see if we were getting snow here! Ha! And Jane and I were saying just watching it come down on TV was making us feel cold.

Maybe seeing Shania Twain at the half will warm you up.

You mean us!

I didn't say that.

But it must be really hard on the southern US boys to play in snow and sub-zero conditions.

They've got to really love the game. Average salary is $80K. $80K!

Huh, when they all hoped to be in the NFL, or were and sent down.

Like our hockey players who end up in Europe or wherever.

Yah, it was really interesting yesterday – watching the Vanier Cup – Did you?

No, I don't follow it.

Right. So the announcer – it was Western University – the Mustangs – Jane's cousin's son played for them – against Le Rouge et Or. The Laval Red and Gold – a really great team – big, fast. Anyway, this announcer started with this is **our** boys playing **our** game for **our** cup – and of course I thought that's probably why we like it so much – in addition to the fact that it's always so 'dramatic', as we were saying. You never know who will win, who'll drop the ball, do something crazy. It's all so much fun.

Who won?

Totally unbelievable! Western blew Laval away. Right from the get-go. 38-10 I think. The end of the Laval dynasty.

Geez.

Yah, seriously, Western played a letter-perfect game.

Sounds great.

Lots of fun.

Right on... So how's the book coming?

I promised Jane I wouldn't talk about it. I have reservations, pun intended.

Spoiler alert?

Ha. Maybe that's it!

Nothin?... Are you serious I'm in it?

Well, yah, in a way. Remember it's fiction though.

So?

So I take a lot of liberty with the truth and you won't be identified and likely at best if you are it would be sort of a 'based on' type of thing…

So how's it going? Solve the great Indian reconciliation thing? Did you get my email about the Inquiry?

Yah, thanks. Will any real change come out of it is the question. Those poor families. Not so far. But I'll say this, seriously: I feel like I am into it in the right direction, if not the level of depth I would like to be at.

Geez, that's pretty philosophical. Or more like a political answer. You're failing to 'show, not tell'?

That's always my Achilles heel.

Huh...

Although there is a character in it who I really like. He's an Indian Agent in the late 1880s. And I like a couple of the poems in it.

Cool.

OK. Enough said. Let's have a wee scotch, a toke and get back down to the game.

And Shania.

Right on! -- Oh yah, and how's the Kerouac book going?

Strange dude hanging out with strange people: Burrows, Ginsberg, some good looking guy – bi – who kills an older gay dude who is stalking him. Kerouac himself seems really proud of his French-Canadian heritage. Good book.

Cool.

So let's see if we can identify the five or six Canadians in the starting lineup.

Ha! No kidding, eh.

you snooze you lose

To:	Ivan
Cc:	
Subject:	you snooze you lose

Hey Ivan,

Big thanks to you and Jane for the great Cup party! Watching football sipping scotch and toked up is pretty far out, for sure. And those wings when the munchies hit! AND right on TO! I had really counted them out when that crazy fumble was recovered and run back. Ah, the entertainment value of sport!

Did a little more checking on the murdered and missing, and remember how it seems many of the murderers knew the girls and women they killed? Well, that was sort of a surprise (or perverse relief that it wasn't always a white predator), but if you listen to some of the families who say they pretended to the police that their daughter/mother/sister was white. WHY? So that the police would act on their notification to the cops. WHY? Because, I am guessing a bit, becuz the police have received so many of these calls that they assume it's JUST another missing aboriginal female who may well end up dead. WHY? Because someone she knows will kill her in some angry/drugged out/fucked up state. WHY? Becuz their culture is virtually destroyed, as I already said, and that's just one example of the death throes of a dying culture. AND, you can't put that back together again. At least I don't think you can, and so here we go round and round again. Good luck, seriously, with an impossible topic to have chosen for your book. Unless you are going to do something really boring or brilliant. Which brings up something else I guess you've already considered.

As you probably heard – who hasn't – Prince Harry is going to marry an American girl, and everybody is agog about it. So how you move from settling the score with Aboriginals to getting rid of the Monarchy altogether is beyond me. People want pageantry and something to talk about that is beyond their mundane reality. Not to mention Trump and us being the 51st State of the US – check out the beating we are taking on soft wood exports – and not to mention Trump and Kim Jong-un in their pissing match, and people now starting to prepare bomb shelters/nuclear survival strategies.

WTF!!

Pete

ps brilliant of course!

WTF

To: Pete

Cc:

Subject: WTF

📎 ⊐ There are times.pdf (126 KB) ⊐ A high raven's.pdf (84 KB) ⊐ COYOTE.pdf (363 KB)

Yes, WTF! It really is crazy out there, and I'm thinking the only way I can tackle the decolonization issue is to somehow tap into a more universal aspect of the manifestation of power over others, as evident in the mindset of colonizers. How's that for a mouthful!

Remember I mentioned finding that journal of the Indian Agent, Beacham? Well, I did more digging on Wiki and found that his son Jerome — who lived to 1980 — became a successful businessman in Winnipeg and had a lot of his father's writings, which were discovered by Jerome's daughter, and that she is planning to publish them. Some are online already and I plan to use some in the book. There's a subtle lament in them for the loss of culture. And the importance of 'place'. Something I found in the work of our Al Purdy. It's not unlike Emily Carr's paintings of the totem poles, documenting what she knew was a rapidly-disappearing way of life — of a dignified culture.

So there's something in that. Something that is not abstract like notions of the 'the nation state', 'transnationalism', 'international corporatism', 'empire', but a human dimension that I'm trying to get at. It's like the notion that there are a bunch of genes that just keep looking for bodies to propagate in — or something like that — but the reverse in a sense: like being — being human or just being itself — moves through so many landscapes, timescapes, dimensions where it is assaulted and loved and wins sometimes and loses and — what? — what then? So I have to find a few simple truths, a few fragments of the essential, hoping that the essential — that essentialness of being human — will sustain victims of any kind of abuse and our kids, and our grandkids — for seven generations (at least) — as the aboriginals say (I think).

So Beacham lived with his Sioux wife, Thachiwan — meaning 'doe' — in the bush near Kenora — and seems to have fully transformed into "Coyote". That must have been just before or about the time Archibald Belaney 'became' "Grey Owl". Here's a couple of his poems (attached) and a chunk from his "I am Coyote" — a long poem.

There are times,

Soft, silent times

When in the forest, alone

In nature, the animals

At the edge of my little

Fire's light

The snow-ladened branches

Bent for the night;

Far away from man, from the madding

crowd,

I can for a moment

Find peace; and remember there is

Still something special

In wilderness, something

Greater than all my kind;

Something of which we are a part.

A high raven's throaty call — awk, awk —

The shrill of a blue jay — cree, cree, creee —

blue sky eternal.

Shadowy evergreens on the distant shore

In the water lily bay

the lazy flowing fading arc of a fishing line

Scintillating rays play a dazzling tune

across the glass surface

Silly water bugs near shore a crazy carnival

of drunken skaters darting, zigging,

colliding, zigging and zagging again,

in silence.

All at home.

I am Coyote, and I know so little;
all that I know is that I am
Coyote.
I was left on the shore.
Left naked on the shore of the Sea of Life and Death.
Naked, and alone — like you are, or
have been, or will be.

When I awoke, that time,
I thought it was true
Enlightenment — of course
there were a thousand questions
for which I had no certain answers,
and a thousand more that I
did not even know to ask:
but even that knowing seemed like
Enlightenment itself — I believed
being in permanent doubt was
what being alive, and awake, was all about.
And there was some comfort in the knowing of that
half-knowing.
I began to look about, feeling good as the
patterns of and in the world
around me became clear — pieces
that had never fit — many pieces — seemed
effortlessly to float around and join others;
and naked though I was, I felt
less alone.

My challenge was before me, it
was more immediate:
what clothing would I
dress in? Who was I, actually?
That this birthing had taken
nearly 30 years was no
concern to me — it seemed natural,
indeed,
earlier attempts at
being had really been role playing,
trying hard to be what my whole world
(which I now know was so small)
wanted me to be while I tried
to carve out some distinctiveness, and
I did go so far on some occasions to
shout out loud my assertion of
who and what I was, what I
would and would not do, to
establish that I was unique.

Now, naked and more truly alone than
I could remember — I thought I would
be a man and that I would spend
my life trying to answer only
those questions which I found important:
I would choose the questions I would answer.

I put on man's clothing and

I left the shore of the Sea of

Life and Death to wonder,

self-centeredly, considering

and rejecting, or accepting, questions that

were worth living to answer.

And I never once thought I was

Coyote.

Did I have any clues, you ask?

Was there any way that I might have

known I was a small wolf?

Perhaps. There were some hints I suppose.

For immediately after awakening on the shore

I sniffed the air, turned from the sea and wandered for

2 years looking for bush land,

thick forest, where I found myself

at ease. And when wandering again,

through fortune, really, I ended a long journey

out on ice flows —

in frozen land with small bushes, large granite boulders

and the great open water

just on the horizon. I

found that there too I was

at ease. And when on another

long trip I came here to Lake of the Woods

I was at home as well.

I could feel the land, the rock-bed of the forest,

the wind-swept trees and

the air in my bones.

So I have kept to the forest now for
these past 30 years. I have seen the
soft woods fall and decay to be replaced
by maple, beech and oak. I know
the wild creatures of the forest and have a
sense of kin toward them.
But I did not know I was Coyote.
Perhaps, likewise, you too have no sense of
who you really are?

There were, in truth, other clues. Other
clues that might be called more
objective.
And as some will say, more
persuasive than my subjective sense of
being drawn to the forest, and so forth.
But I am getting ahead of myself on
two points. One, that these objective clues
'staring me in the face' existed, and
what they were. And two, that they should somehow
have been more obvious to me, more
instructive. More influential in coming to
know that I am Coyote.

I will come to these eventually. For after all,
they too
are

just

phenomena now long past yet

easy enough to recall, living

fragments of

who I am. Important pieces

of a pattern. Not the

pattern

itself.

Living in the forest is not easy;

I never believed it was for everyone.

Growing and killing the food you eat

hauling the water you drink

felling the trees and chopping

the wood for your fire's heat,

trapping, tanning and selling animal pelts;

being

cut off

being

shut-in by the snow

hearing the winds howl

and feeling them shake your house

living

in absolute

darkness

when the sun

goes down, your only

light the moon and stars —

long, long

silences — a

death-like silence

which distorts

time,

time distorted by menial survival tasks

without end and

a trip to the

outside world

a crossing over

to a **very** other reality.

When weeks have become months

and months years

and years

decades

there is no

reason to

doubt your nature;

or if you do,

to deny that which

you must have needed to do.

Even when I tried to conform

people could see through me they

might have wanted to embrace

me — because I was attractive

in a strange way; I had

something to

offer — and I gave and

they took, and I

took back some too

but

there was a veil, a

gulf we could not bridge

and seldom were there

hard feelings.

After all, I found my

viscera churning and

wanting to be attuned

to the rhythm of man.

I felt the pain of

Mankind, especially my Indian brothers and

I was motivated almost exclusively

by a need to heal the pain —

then —

years later, after years of

going out into

the world from the bush —

I returned there to heal myself.

You may ask

wasn't the forest just

a hide-a-way for Thachiwan, Jerome and myself, not

the centre of my being?

I began to think so.
I began to see what I did
as just that: what I did — just like
I grant you to do and be
what it is you do.

But then I began to ask myself
whether what I did, whether who or
what I was, was
authentic.

I began to look much
deeper
than
when I had first decided
life was an opportunity to choose and
answer the questions which only we
find worthy of asking.
The way I had seen it,
life was full of
problems that needed
solutions: feeding and sheltering ourselves;
buying and selling goods and services;
inventing,
educating,
caring for those
in pain — and it was up
to each of us to decide

what type of problems
we wished to
solve.

It was as though we could
trust our upbringing,
and whatever
special influences in our lives —
and we each would do
that which is
natural
to us.

That whatever I did was also to
be authentic never
crossed my
mind in
that sort of deliberate
way.

For years.

The years continued to
pass and I
had glimpses of
my totem —
one day,

returning from the world
of pain,
I met a brush wolf
standing still, and calm,
watching me long before I
had seen him, staring at me
with friendly eyes
holding my gaze, unmoving,
until I passed.

And
I
took
note of this.

I began to
study this brush wolf
who had been in the forest
with me all these many
years and I had
not
known him.

And then one time, as I
was gaining ascendancy
in the world, with the
deep-rooted

respect of Indian people,

I was being treated

as a wolf, even Thachiwan

said I was a

wolf — a timber wolf —

or even a great silver wolf —

the alpha wolf.

When a

medicine man

prayed for all of us in

the mountains,

when

he prayed the prayer of

Coyote I could feel

the spirit descend like

a great wild beast howling, the screeching howl

rolling down the

rocky mountains

shaking every creature, shaking the forest and every rock

on the way

and everything in the valley

below with us

that day.

And I took

note.

I believed I

was in contact

with Coyote.

Not long after,

my heart was saddened.

I found my brush wolf

pacing at the

roadside, sniffing

his mate

who lay dead,

torn and broken

in the ditch.

My brush wolf pacing, running

away a short distance, afraid, confused,

stricken; and then

darting back to his mate;

and he looked at me just for a moment,

sniffed her again

and turned

to disappear

in the thick bush.

And I took

note.

I mourned

the loss of

his love,

and I asked

others after him, but he remained
hidden.

Death, it seemed, was in
the air. Death out in the world, Death
at the forest's edge.
Levels of pain
and death
too much for
anyone to endure.

So I turned deeper into
the forest once again.
I gave up trapping
and I worked with wood.
I grew to know wood more than
I thought possible.
I found the sun's rays
trapped for years inside wood,
running in golden shards
through the grains of maple
and yellow birch;
I felt the cold marble-like
smoothness of sanded hardwood
that has been
hand-rubbed
with walnut oil.

I discovered
patience and
peace
in my work
with wood.

It came as a surprise,
then, when
Death touched me
at my work one
sunny afternoon.

It was just a shadow — a
slow-moving darkness, a chilling
that crossed between me
and the sun at my back.
I looked up,
turned to face the sun,
called out,
looked through the trees far overhead,
but it was gone.
And I
took
note.

I knew it
was Death.

Was I afraid, you ask?
Yes, sometimes.

Did I change my behaviour?
Yes, but I knew that more
was required of me.

Did I not, you ask, realize
by now that I was Coyote?

No.

Sometimes death's sting
is so sudden
we are left
stupefied, we
are left instantly
in a thick fog where
just seconds ago there
was the light of
a life — now snuffed
out — gone without
farewells, without
reconciliation for words
we said and
regret for past deeds of wrongdoing
that cannot be
broached — there is

no

more

communication — the

vault of death is

sealed, beyond our

grasp and forever a

breach in our

soul's longing

to connect just one

more time, if only

for a second.

Sometimes death lingers;

first it is noticed

as a stranger — a

hint of alienation in the

form of a little complaint,

an ailment, a series of

unexplained symptoms that

refuse to go away — a vague sense of

erosion, of the decaying

of health, a tipping

of internal

balances

which becomes a

turning, a downward

slide into restrictions,

fatigue, loss of joy,

serious impairment and

then

disability;

a withdrawal of

energy, of life

forces, and

a steady engulfment

of darkness,

of lonely

solitary

entrapment;

and the world around us —

the sun, birds,

the sounds of gaiety, of

life

grow more and more

remote

as death

progresses on its

march,

onwards now

with growing momentum —

weeks, months, and

years after

it was only a hint

it takes over — a putrid stench

at our deathbed, ready now to

close the door

on another
victim.

It was like that
for me, except
lying by my fire one day,
beaten down,
nearly lifeless
I drifted into
a zone that was
a nameless
state where death
is certain and life
improbable, almost totally gone.

I do not know why,
no one does,
no one ever does:
I awoke, all of my
Being,
all that was left
was concentrated
in my middle eye
and I knew I had
been spared.

And slowly, one small
step at a time

I began the journey
of recovery; I
grew from a point of
consciousness and
a barely living thing, weak,
unsteady, uncertain
of my step
unaware of the road
ahead
just able to put one foot
in front of the other, one
careful step
at a
time.

It will soon be
two full years since
I was touched
by the
Grim Reaper;
and yes, of course
I have changed.

Some like me less.
Some like me more.
Many, as before, remain indifferent.

What matters now is I
have a sense of destiny.

I awoke today and I
know that I am
Coyote.

If you want, you will
find me.

(Excerpt of the Collected Works of William Beacham, 1910)

<no subject>

To:	Ivan
Cc:	
Subject:	<no subject>

Wow, I get the place thing but maybe it's time you stopped writing and started ranting on YouTube.

Seriously. What did I hear recently? Millennials have about a 15 minute attention span. And things are moving so quickly books are just too slow to deal with any contemporary issue. Especially something so ingrained/systemic as the exploitation of indigenous people – the importance of 'place' – not to mention apocalyptic Trump and Kim Jong-un.

I think I'm going to put Stephane Grapelli on, smoke a joint and sip some wine. And not to be too flippant – enjoy my 'place' here on the river while I can.

WTF,
Your Bro Pete.

get mine

To:	Ivan
Cc:	
Subject:	get mine

Did you?

get mine

To: Pete
Cc:
Subject: get mine

Yes I did. I've been struggling with blind alleys and dead ends. And your apocalyptic stuff got very real when Jodi visited recently. She's 12 for Christ's sake. So I wrote these and want to turn the corner in the book. Rant later.

I'm honoured

But I'm also pissed off that

Jodi, 12 years old and

Admittedly precocious and

Too smart for her own good

Sidles up to me as we walk the beach

On Vancouver Island,

Says, "Grandpa, can I interview you

Because I like to get the thoughts of

Different people I don't necessarily believe everything they say

And won't automatically act on what they advise me to do but I find

I do learn a lot by listening", and she asks me:

"Am I likely to experience the apocalypse in my time?"

In one breath I'm shocked she'd ask this and in another

It's not surprising because of course she's so adult and taking so much in

From the Zombie Apocalypse to hearing her father and mother

Talk about making preparations for a nuclear attack from North Korea and

I feel sad we've come to this. I'm pissed off we've come to this.

I'm feeling impotent we've come to this.

But I don't want her to know that

I think it's possible

And that at my age having fought a relatively good fight and 'kept the faith'

I still feel that humanity is indeed fucked up and doing about all it

Can to kill life as we know it despite

Many great efforts to the contrary –

So I think it's possible even accounting for

My chronic deep pessimism that I always try to

Not just philosophically rise above but

Existentially, erotically, and manage 99% of the time

And want her to have the same odds and experience the same

Joie de vivre that I have

And the long good loving life that her grandmother and I have had and so I

Lie.

"I don't think so, Jodi. I think we could have some limited nuclear war

Or environmental disaster than might break up the world into

Little pockets cut off from one another,

Having to make adjustments to survive by what's available locally

And slowly managing to evolve rather

Than a complete apocalypse."

"Ohhh", she says.

I can hear the wheels turning.

We walk on in silence, closer

Than we have been for years.

Bedrock and stone are my spine they're

my bones,

soil is my flesh

water my blood

air my breath.

The earth is my body

and it has been pierced and scarred

torn, hammered, flooded, choked

and burned, stripped, mined

and abused.

The earth is my body

my temple

my home:

it has struggled and strained

been broken and worked to the bone

been held captive,

treated as chattel,

bought and sold –

And I am not alone

I am not alone

Jodi

To: Ivan
Cc:
Subject: Jodi

Jesus. Time to rant man.

P

You want rant?

To:	Pete
Cc:	
Subject:	You want rant?

📎 ⊼ Memories.pdf (94 KB)   ⊼ Cranmer's Potlatch.jpg (2.1 MB)   ⊼ Carr, Alert Bay 1928.pdf (188 KB)   ⊼ So Cool.pdf (234 KB)

So Pete I'm getting depressed with the bleak prospects for Canada's First Nations. And with the 51st State of the USA shit and with what we are dumping on Jodi and her generation. You can't deal with the decolonization of Canada only by saying you are going to decolonize FNs – you have to cut with the Crown and the Eagle. Get rid of the hangover of Empire. So the answer has to be found in the heart of Canadians themselves. To face their own fears and embrace a new vision which includes a genuine respect for FNs and a new alignment.

I'm attaching four pieces that will find their way into the book. The first is a set of memories I have of things that were said to me by American colleagues who I thought – and still do think – of as decent, professional, caring people. They were said I think in some cases when these people had forgotten I was Canadian.

And I'm attaching a picture taken in Alert Bay in 1921 of wonderful artwork and carvings forcibly taken from Dan Cranmer at his potlatch by Indian Agent William Halliday. I accompany it with a little story of Emily Carr's visit to Alert Bay in 1928.

And while I fully intend to turn the corner I've thrown in something I wrote called So Cool.

Our busy day working at the UN over we

sat down to dinner at the Beekman Tower, where diplomats hang out;

my treat, to host my American colleague, the head of our group.

And when the conversation turned to Canada

and Quebec's growing desire to separate

she interrupted me without apology and said,

"We won't let that happen."

"What?" I asked, a little stunned.

"The USA won't let Quebec break up Canada."

And that was that.

Ten years later, in 1994, as the referendum on separation

was all the talk, and gravely so,

I was reassured by my American colleagues as we sipped beer

and played poker

deep in Sudan

that I need not worry about it: the USA would send a couple of fighter planes over and people in

Quebec would get the message.

Introduced to one of my
American heroes in the
field of conflict resolution,
he shook my hand and said,
"A Canadian.
That's the country
that thinks it is an NGO."

The American Ambassador spoke Spanish
to my colleague when I was introduced,
saying I
did not speak Spanish.
She said, "Canadians, nice people
but they have no pistola."

TOURIST TO EMILY CARR, CAMPBELL RIVER HOTEL 1928:

I'm telling you he was only doing his job

that William Halliday and it was about time

the Feds gave the Indian Agents some authority

to do the dirty work the politicians in Ottawa

and the Churches want done,

to get rid of that potlatch, the way it stands in the path

of progress, of democracy, of getting the Indians

free of their old ways and up to speed.

EMILY:

Huh.

TOURIST:

Right. Some of the stuff they do is crazy anyway,

those masks and poles all to do with the animal world, spirits and

strange beliefs and how giving a shitload of gifts to people and

putting on a spectacle with dancing like crazy, possessed people

was doing them any good. Really!

EMILY:

Uh, huh.

TOURIST:

So what if a whole bunch of them that wouldn't give it up ended

in Oakalla

and that Dan Cranmer's party was spoiled –

maybe it was wrong then for Halliday to try to sell that stuff and
how it all ended up in museums and private collections
as far away as the States, on the east coast.

(pause)

Maybe there was some artistic value to it. Or novelty.
Or as someone with a mouthful said, anthropological significance.

EMILY:
Right.

TOURIST:
Anyway, what's done is done.
Time to move on.

EMILY (under her breath):
Damned tourists!

I'd like to be so cool

Chaos cud swirl about me

The fires of human suffering

Cud burn and threaten to

Engulf me

The emptiness of eternity

Cud beckun to me

Like Mermaids, Irresistible Sirens,

Like a raven's call in

The Northwest

Wilderness

And

My Self,

Disappeared,

Wud

Just

Be

Gone.

I'd be so cool.

The pools of human

And animal

Suffering

Wud

Rise up,

Rise up to my knees

My waist

My chest

My throat

My nostrils;

And instead of smothering me

I'd be so cool

So cool –

Even the coolest tribal elders,

The Giant Gorillas and clever orangutans

And ancient trees

Still standing and watching in silence,

The Shamans

And medicine women

The truthsayers –

Those who know –

Wud

Nod

To me,

The coolest human

They had met.

And

I

Wuddnt

Write about it.

I

Wuddnt

Talk about it.

How COOL wud that be.

I do not want to cry for Canada

for so many people who were here first,

who made their homes in rough and unforgiving wilderness

and were killed, their entire cultures

pulverized under the steady persistent grinding machine of explore,

conquer, and exploit; the machine of Empire.

I do not want to cry for Canada

for desperate, determined, well-meaning settlers

escaping punishing poverty or yet again another

form of oppression by the machinations of gluttony

that cares not one hoot for the little guy.

I do not want to cry for Canada

for millions of buffalo killed with impunity in an obscene

slaughter that knew no limits conducted for unbridled profit and

frontier entertainment by even the most civilized Europeans

seeking adventure, thrill and

trophies to mount on the walls of their lakeside estates.

I do not want to cry for Canada

for family-owned businesses started

as an act of faith, a hopeful response to a human drive

for self-respect and moderate success in towns and cities

where people knew one another, nodded a hello when they met on

the street, came together to celebrate birth and put the dead to rest

with dignity.

I do not want to cry for Canada
for a farm team and branch plant mentality that seeks
validation in the United States of America
and fails to foster, embrace and celebrate
excellence but rather contents itself with keeping
things calmly mediocre while secretly harkening to the slightest
inflections of every star it has produced,
uncomfortable with the competitive instinct
that fuels the best in the world.

I do not want to cry for Canada
for having been colonized and
having embedded within it the deep impulse to
be a colonizer itself, acting as the victim who often
when liberated becomes the victimizer,
harbouring the pride and prejudice of what
shaped, sometimes stripped, and
left it what it is.

I do not want to cry for Canada.
Ohhh Canada
I do not want to cry for you.

Who paints the place today?

Who is the 2017 Group of Seven – and the Tom Thompson,

the Emily Carr, Norval Morriseau – *Copper Thunder*?

Who writes the poetry of Canada?

Where is today's Pauline Johnson,

Al Purdy, Milton Acorn?

Who tells the stories of ordinary Canadians?

The Roch Carrier, Pierre Burton and Peter C. Newman?

Who sings the songs of Canada today?

Where is today's Stan Rogers, The Hip, Stompin' Tom?

What is the place today?

How does the place look? Sound?

Who *feels* the place today and celebrates it

like the old timers?

Where is the frontier today?

The wilderness?

The untamed waters and blinding blizzards?

The wild animals that send shivers down your spine

at the thought of meeting them in the bush?

Where are the places of complete silence?

Of darkness so dark you cannot see three feet in front of you?

Where is Canada?

What is the soul of Canada these days, in 2017?

What Rocky Mountains have yet to be scaled, can't be scaled?

What virgin timber yet to be cut, won't be cut?

What mineral yet to be mined, will never be mined?

What fish or sea creature yet to be caught, won't be caught?

What place where no man has been, there'll be no footprints?

What and where is pristine?

Where is the path to the heart of Canada?

that's heavy shit

To:	Ivan
Cc:	
Subject:	that's heavy shit

Hey, how's the book coming? And what you up to Xmas and NY?

that's heavy shit

To:	Pete
Cc:	
Subject:	that's heavy shit

```
The whole family here but all quiet for NY. Pushing on the book,
pissing Jane off I'm not Xmas shopping. You?
```

that's heavy shit

To:	Ivan
Cc:	
Subject:	that's heavy shit

We laying low too. Like all the energy has gone out of 2017, cocooning and waiting for someone to get rid of Trump any way possible.

Here's another one for you:
Don't worry about old age. It doesn't last long.

Best,
Pete

A. J. Hoffman 2017

The spider's web
Is neatly woven
The strands are made of
Cultures cast in
Life's great oven
And in each culture
The signs are drawn,
A language spoken,
Woven together and forged
In the light of dawn
They should not be broken.

Then comes a hollow man
Whose heart has been stolen
Right at birth or when
His spirit was still molten
A desperado easy for the taking
A King, a Lord or an Idea
His life it would be making;
His hands, his sword, his gun,
His mind and his being
Are far from solid, inside are shaking
As in the service of Empire
He wields power over innocent others
Who now are also quaking.

There is no hope
In this perverse mirrored existence

Of strength appropriated

And feeble resistance

No way desperados beholden to Empire

Can break from that which breaks them

Until near the point at which they expire

A leavening comes not in the daylight

But at the midnight hour.

There the strands of being human

Of something more than savage

If perchance they exist and in the heart beat still

Arise from within the darkness

And forge again a newfound will,

A will resolute and loving

Knowing that great schemes of Kings and Lords and Ideas

Cannot surpass or undermine the place

Of grounded being, whether

In the valley, on the plain, or atop the hill.

Place we are and Place we shall remain:

Place to which we go,

Place we are right now,

And Place from which we came;

It is Place that feeds and shelters us

Place we sing and write about

Place that shapes our culture and

Place from which we take our name.

The spider's web
Is neatly woven
The strands are made of
Cultures cast in
Life's great oven
And in each culture
The signs are drawn,
A language spoken,
Woven together and forged
In the light of dawn
They should not be broken.

So catch and trap evil, save us from Empire schemers;
Let our dreams pass through and keep us dreamers –
Raise our voices in freedom celebration,
A chant, a ballad or some great ovation;
Strengthen our connection to the past
Make real the sense of belonging,
Cast our eyes into the heavens and
Dare to live in peace on earth, live
Life without the desperado's longing.

Nobody could beat the Russians and the USSR:
from Sputnik 1 in '57 to Yuri Gagarin, first cosmonaut in space in
'61 the great US of A played catch-up and
all of us in the free world
dreaded the spread of Communism, feared nuclear war
and lived in awe or watched transfixed as our athletes faced
superhumans who came from behind the Iron Curtain
with bodies perfectly honed, faces of stone
and a mechanical determination to
out-run, out-ski, out-swim, out-skate
everyone.

But there was one game that was our game – hockey –
Canada's game – and we weren't about to
lose it to the Ruskies, the Reds, the Commies.
1972.
The Summit Series, The Super Series, The Canada-USSR Series.
Russia came to play the best in the world. Our Pros. And they were
ordered to win, but not by too much
so as to embarrass the weak West.
An eight game series. Four in Canada. Four in Russia.
The eyes of the world watching.
West meets East.
Capitalism meets Communism.
Freedom meets Captivity.
And Team Canada named no one Captain.
How much more Canadian can you get?

Hockey icon Foster Hewitt returned from retirement
to announce the play-by-play on TV in his quintessential nasal
voice, that "Hello Canada and Hockey fans in the United States and
Newfound"… that "It's Hockey Night in Canada!" voice. The voice we
all wanted to ring out the words, "he shoots, he scores!" as another
Canadian shot blows past the Russian goalie.
But someone, indeed everyone, had underestimated the systematic,
virtually robotic team play of no-name Soviets
whose physical fitness, stamina, emotional discipline,
and finely-tuned skating, passing, puck-handling and shooting
skills made it look as though the Reds were going to
destroy the Canucks.
When at a moment of extreme low Phil Esposito, one of Canada's
four non-Captains, one of the Alternates, looked the camera in the
eye and spoke these words to every Canadian glued to the TV,
watching in a state of loss and shock: "We are not here for the
money or fame *but because we love Canada.*"

Then it turned.
Not without a battle royal that forced each man to dig deeper than
he had ever dug, and not before each man joined in union at a
transcendent level with every other player
and the team was unbeatable,
the Paul Henderson goal scored on a
Phil Esposito rebound that will never be forgotten,
three Russian defenders caught forever
in a frozen state of shock as their incredible goalie Vladislav Tretiak

lay splayed on the ice as

Cournoyer and Henderson embraced each other in the incomparable

joy of monumental victory, mere men who fought

the Russian Bear with the ferocity and intensity of a cornered

animal. The Canadian way of playing the Canadian game.

Of course, Canadians everywhere went wild.

We were indeed the best in the world.

We had scored an historic victory for freedom and democracy.

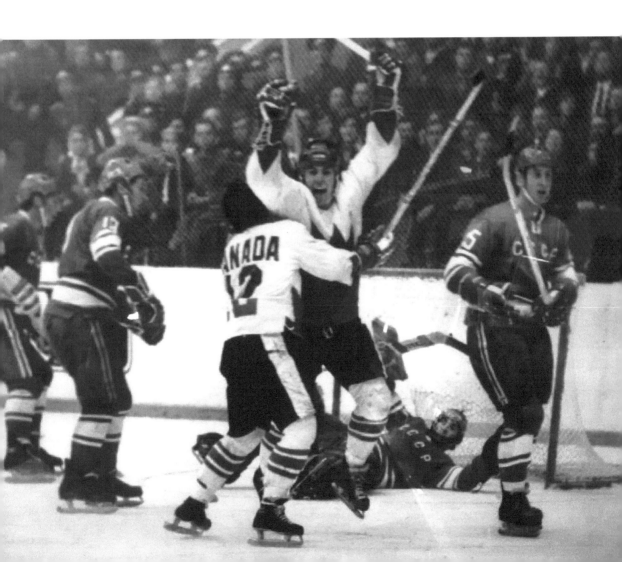

But, 28 years later,

could we defeat the mighty USA

who had now come to claim

the game as theirs?

The place?

Vancouver.

The occasion?

The 2010 Winter Olympics, the Gold Cup final.

The TV audience:

22 million, that's two of every three Canadians and 27 million
Americans, the most watched hockey game in the USA in 30 years.

The set-up?

Canada lost to the USA in the preliminary round. A 5–3 defeat.
Every Canadian watching was anxious. Could our boys do it?
Could the mouse roar and beat the elephant? Do we Canucks have
the can-do, will-do, did-do? Is hockey still deep in our genes?
Is it still *our* game?

The play-by-play?

A dramatic gigantic struggle of two nations pitted against each other
on the shoulders of their born and bred red-blooded American and
Canadian men. The Canucks fighting to defend a 2–1 lead, with
every Canadian holding their breath, counting the seconds to victory:
30, 29, 28, 27, 26… and the USA scored!

And Canadians everywhere slumped, sighed, shook themselves,
inhaled and regrouped as the Gold Cup game went into overtime.

Syd the Kid from Cole Harbour Nova Scotia:

There is no accounting for magnificence. In Canada we know it comes from every corner of this huge country. And we mere mortals who don't have the stuff can only imagine what it is to be the best in the world. The BEST! So here we go… it's sudden death overtime in the Gold Cup game of the 2010 Winter Olympics, Canada versus the USA…

Fly, Check, Dig

We have to win

I have to score

Got the puck

Drive for the net

Shoot to his top left

Go, go, go

Break through the defence

Fuck I'm checked

Get it

Get it out of the corner

Get it out

Flip it out

Push for the net

It's on my stick

Shoot!

It's in –

– It's in –

Yes it's in!

We've won – we've won –

We've WON!

Syd the Kid from Cole Harbour fired a lightning-fast shot,
A golden shot
And the crowd went nuts.
Canadians poured into the streets,
From coast to coast to coast,
from pubs and sports bars and house parties
filling the streets in a swell of national pride and joy,
cars circling the downtown of every town and city in Canada,
the car horns blasting
people walking around in ecstasy, waving the Canadian flag,
shaking each other's hands,
hi-fiving one another,
the nation united
in victory
small groups assembling spontaneously
to sing our national anthem –

OH CANADA
OH CANADA
OUR HOME AND NATIVE LAND.
OH CANADA
THE TRUE NORTH STRONG AND FREE.

Nothing like this in the past
60 years.
Nothing like it since the end of World War Two.
Nothing.

We had always struggled to define our identity

As in what we are

Not want we aren't

We knew all too well and cherished

What we weren't

Starting with American;

And we hunted for it, debated it,

Tried to name it mosaic,

Canuck,

Describe it tolerant,

Diverse, peace-loving and

Peace-keeping.

We were the beaver, the moose,

The maple leaf,

The Canada Goose,

The Group of Seven

Terry Fox

Ann Murray

Margaret Atwood

Bell and Banting,

Reid and Carr,

Cohen, Dion, and Twain,

Orr, Gretzky, Crosby,

Young and KD Lang,

Ackroyd

And Short,

Myers and

Shatner and

Michael J. Fox.

The CBC

The Grey Cup

Canada Day and

Everything hockey:

The symbols, the stars and the

Fibres that bound us together

In our sparsely-populated

Magnificent country

That we loved in a

Quiet, deprecating

Canadian way.

Time rolled on.

The clock struck midnight.

Our 150-year-old country

turned a calendar year older and before us stretched two paths,

the one brave and the other bolder.

On the first for years we tried so very hard to keep the family ties

that bind and we clung to the idea of the home team

even as our boys and girls followed a thin threaded path

toward the top that crossed borders into foreign cultures

that were eroding just like ours, slipping away in a transnational

corporatism, the homogenization of identity

driven by the concentration of wealth manipulating a cyber world so

that a virtual reality of being Haida, or Quebequois, a Canuck –

a palpable extract or distillation of

what it was to be Haida, Quebequois, Canuck – was *in fact*

a remote memory of a feeling as though

you were in touch with an ancient ancestor

from which you could try hard to grasp an

indescribable

grounding,

a grounding as though you *really* had the stuff of

the sea-to-sea-to-sea,

the Canadian Shield,

the vast Prairie,

the frozen north and the raw

awesome Rocky Mountains in your blood,

in your DNA –

while the Family,

the Tribe,

and State

withered away.

It all withered away

As deep time,

Time that has always been,

Time before colonization,

Time before First Nation,

Time before the birth of civilization

before homo sapien,

Time before the dinosaur

before the Seven Seas,

Time before the sun and the moon and the stars,

Deep Time swallowed

everything.

The other path demanded that we be much bolder

Seen here at the midnight hour

When future gazing is still within our power

Recalls our poet Cohen who said, "it is murder"

But can we look a little further,

Beyond the Family and the Tribe

Beyond Nation, Empire and its destructive power,

Can Canada shed its colonial skin

Hold out a beacon that shines from deep within

From a heart that will not abide injustice

Where evil dreams are caught and yet dreamers we remain,

Dreaming in a place well-grounded

No Kings, no Lords, no Ideas our freedom will contain;

Where Canada's web is neatly woven

The strands are made of cultures cast in life's great oven

A country forged in the light of dawn,

A place that will not break nor be broken;

Where Deep Time may be the Grim Reaper

But Canadians do not sleep in fear

There is another drum we hear

And the dreams we dream

Inspire hope and ignite the flames

Of a people made safe by the dream catcher,

Knowing that skin colour, the roads we each have travelled

To this place, all our names, the signs we make

And the songs we sing

And the important ways we each find meaning

On the frontier of the unknown really do matter,

And that we are made better by using power with

And not over one another?

One path is for the brave,

The other for the bolder

As Canada turns another year older.

Here it is

To:	Pete
Cc:	
Subject:	Here it is

Hey Pete. As promised. Many thanks, and Happy New Year,

Your bro,

Ivan

ps now it's time to rant

Photos and Maps

Page 15: The graphic of the many uses of buffalo is courtesy of the South Dakota State Historical Society.

Page 16: Tribal distributions at time of contact map. Oblatesinthewest.library.ualberta.ca

Page 26: Map of Canada showing Rupert's Land. See Sunnyside Historical Society, Parkdale, Toronto.

Page 28: Aerial view of Cree Land, Gogama, from *Google Earth*.

Page 34: Canada from Space is courtesy of the Royal Canadian Geographical Society.

Pages 38–39: Scoop-roofed shanty and Squared log house are respectively on the farm of Wilhelm Budd, Wilberforce Township and August Tabbert, Alice Township as found in *Harvest of Stones*, Brenda-Lee Whiting, University of Toronto Press. 1985.

Pages 42–43: On the shore of the lake Kutenai, from the Edward S. Curtis Collection (Library of Congress), no. 3188-10, c.1910.

Page 53: The photo of buffalo skulls is from *Wikipedia*.

Page 67: Scalping Big Mouth. Photo by ethnographer E. S. Curtis. See Smithsonian and The North American Indian, curtis.library.northwestern.edu.

Pages 68–69: The 'before and after' photo of young Thomas Moore, 1874 (Indian name unkown) at the Ou'Appelle School, Saskatchewan can be found as a National Post Photo but appears in many places online – reference especially Canadian residential schools. (wherearethechildren.ca/en/exhibition). The photo of the Cree father with his 'after' children is also online in the discussion of residential schools.

Pages 72–73: The photo of the mill at Balaclava is courtesy of Kris Hoffman, and the deserted fishing village can be found online in searches for Ghost Towns in Canada. The 1930s ghost town (pages 78–79) is online in the public domain.

Page 84: The two kids playing hockey in freezing weather is a photo of Benny Hoffman and Johnny Kohls which appeared in the *Pembroke Observer* on January 3, 1958. Johnny kept a copy and kindly provided it for use in this book.

Page 129: Beach at Metchosin, Vancouver Island.

Page 133: Alberta oil sands, Dan Prat, istockphoto.com

Pages 140–141: Dan Cranmer's potlatch, confiscated by Indian Agent William Halliday. Image D-02021 courtesy of the Royal BC Museum and Archives.

Pages 144–145: 2017 map of Canada, 123rf.com

Page 157: Henderson's Goal. Iconic photo available in public domain, author's copy, and see https://teamcanada1792.ca/media

Art

Page 64: Grey Owl (2005) watercolour/ink media by A.J. Hoffman.

Page 89: Tanoo, Queen Charlotte Islands (1913) by Emily Carr – Image PDP2145 courtesy of the Royal BC Museum and Archives.

Page 151: Dream Catcher (2017) watercolour/gouache by A.J. Hoffman.

Credits

While this book is a work of fiction, it could not have been written without drawing on a range of rich factual and hearsay accounts. The author and publisher wish to give credit for this much-appreciated body of work available online to the researcher and curious reader who could quite easily become happily lost in wonderful, and at times disturbing, stories and characters that have shaped Canada as we find it today. If someone, or some source, has been missed please accept our apology.

Some general information was gleaned from the *Canadian Encyclopaedia* and *Wikipedia*. The segment on Grey Owl meeting King George was modified from an account found in Canadianicon.org (see Dicksen 1973:249). The excerpts from William Beacham's private diary were informed by background information drawn from the CBC's story, *A Slow Death*, see: https://www.cbc.ca/history. An excellent account of hunting buffalo can be found on websites including Head Smashed In Buffalo Jump Alberta. The list of Indigenous names of boys and girls, including Thachiwan, was garnered from INAC websites as well as names lists, including those of the Lakota and Cree. Some of the elements of the fictionalized activities of Raddison and des Groseilliers were found on CBC sites as well as *Canadian Encyclopedia*. The Hockey stories were adapted from accounts on Team Canada's official website (https://teamcanada1792.ca/media) and sports stories in the news, as well as the author's memory.

Special thanks to Peter Sattelberger, Rich Corman, Evelyn Voigt, Anami, Jerome Berthelette, Kevin Hoffman, Evan Hoffman, and Gavin and Pam Ward for outstanding editing and design work.

Cover Art and Design
Kevin Hoffman

Design and Copy Editing
Gavin Ward Design Associates

Dream Catching Canada

ISBN: 9 780986 490750

Published by CIIAN (www.ciian.org)

This book is a historical fiction comprising stories, poems and
images. Some of the characters described are fictional, together
with several real people whose names appear in segments that
are either imaginary or rendered poetically. Fact and fiction are
blended throughout, with no intention to suggest that any of
the text is completely factually correct. Nor is there any intent to
misrepresent or damage the character of anyone, living or not.

Other Books by Ben Hoffman

Conflict, Power and Persuasion: Negotiating Effectively (1990)

The Search for Healing, Reconciliation and the Promise of Prevention (1995)

1+1= 3: New Math for Human Relations (2003)

The Peace Guerilla Handbook (2007)

Peace Guerilla: unarmed and in harm's way, my obsession with ending violence (2010)

Peaceweaving: Shamanistic insights into mediating the transformation of power (2013)

The Hope of Anarchy (2013)

The Violence Vaccine (2016)

CPSIA information can be obtained
at www.ICGtesting.com
Printed in the USA
LVHW072033291118
598712LV00004B/7/P